DAMNED IF I DON'T

Short thrills

Dear Ilda

Many thanks for your kind support

ANT RICHARDS

Hope you enjoy these stories

Ant Richards

ISBN: 1548781169
ISBN-13: 978-1548781163

Also by Ant Richards

In Your Dreams

To Barbara Norma
The more I see you, the more I miss you

And you went that extra mile:

Betty Agostini – you opened the floodgates

Gregorio Tomassi, Judy Donovan, Mariela Mason, Angela
Peddar – you have hearts of gold

Fiona Clark – you're more than just my niece

Xavier Fernandez, Jason Marcellin, Nathaniel Nuby – my
brothers from different mothers

SEVEN SHORT THRILLS

1   The logical outcome

2   Full circle

3   He climbed out through the bathroom window

4   The sentence

5   Málaga Virgen

6   The devil you know

7   No easy answer

Also by Ant Richards

Acknowledgment

About the author

The Logical Outcome

Yesterday, the headaches punished me relentlessly. I can't remember them ever being this bad. Time just seemed to stop, while pain and discomfort increased disproportionately.

Time. This is something I seem to have in abundance. Too much for my own good.

Thinking. Now, that I do quite a lot. However, I always end up digressing. It's what happens when you think too much. Imagine filling up a paper bag with marbles. Then, the bag breaks, scattering the marbles with a confusing rattle on a concrete floor. That's how it feels.

I remember things, then I try to focus, get a grip of the idea and then it happens. The paper bag inside my head breaks and all my thoughts run amok and I get confused. In the end, I just give up on thinking.

To be honest, lately, I have given up on most things.

Even living.

Today, however, I woke up feeling quite light. I had a pleasant enough sleep. As far as I can remember, I only woke up eight times, which is good in a way, because some nights I don't even get to sleep at all.

Yesterday was different. I was miserable, grumpy, and hardly felt like eating anything. Worse still, Geraldine Joy, that stupid cow, didn't turn up, so I had no one to play Snakes & Ladders with. The other nurses never have time for that.

That is why I love Geraldine Joy.

She is patient and very gentle. She sometimes plays a game of Snakes & Ladders and speaks to me very sweetly. She also has a big, sexy rear. Boy, if I were thirty years younger I would date this woman. Well, probably not. Denise would have still been alive and probably wouldn't approve of it.

Denise, you can't imagine how much I miss you!

Anyway, now that she's dead, I am sure she wouldn't mind if I dated Geraldine Joy.

I probably should have started dating and meeting other women after I mourned Denise.

Oh dear! Here I go, digressing again.

Anyway, I am actually feeling much better. The headache is gone. My thoughts are more fluid. I am thinking coherently. In fact, I haven't felt so good since I suffered this damn stroke five years ago.

Here I've been laying, confined to a wheelchair, unable to talk properly, dependant on others to tend to me. It's like being inside this tunnel watching, slowly and painfully, as the outside world cruelly drifts away from me, making it darker and darker.

Now that I come to think about it, I haven't seen my grandchildren in weeks. I wonder why Laura and Geoff don't bring them to see me more often.

Celine, she is such a sweetheart, reminds me of Laura as a child. Liam, the little devil looks just like me. He does take after Geoff in a way – he is my son after all – but it seems when it came to handsomeness, it skipped a generation.

Still, I haven't seen them for a while. I wonder if my son is cross at me. Last time they were here I couldn't remember their names. It happens occasionally; I mix people and names up, forget things.

I better turn round and pull the cord to call the nurses. I want my breakfast now.

Oh shit, what the hell is going on here?

Oh my God! My toes, they're wriggling!

I need to call the nurses.

I can sit.

'Hey!'

Actually... hang on a second, let me try something.

My oh my... these toes are wriggling. Oh dear, I do need to get these toenails cut!

My leg. It moves.

'Hey... nurse!'

I just heard myself!

Wait! Maybe I'm overreacting here. Let's calm the fuck down.

'Nurse!'

Shit, what do you do in these situations?

'Nurse.'

Right ... I must stay calm.

Oh, damn it! It's shit like this that gives you a heart attack and then kills you! Something the bleeding stroke didn't manage five years ago!

Hmm, I can sit up, with some effort, but certainly without pain. Now, this is unusual and scary. So, what do you do in situations like these?

Panic, I guess.

Still, there is no pain.

Gosh! I've managed to put my feet on the floor. I just have to dodge the small side railing fixed to my bed so I don't fall off.

Well, I am sitting straight, my feet firmly planted on the floor. I haven't fallen off the bed.

Now, I just have to take all this in, slowly and one thing at a time.

Ok, it's time to get a bit bolder. Deep breath; don't think too much, just bloody go for it.

Let's stand up.

Crap!

Back on my bum again!

No surprise there, I haven't been very mobile for the past five years now, have I?

Ok, second try.

Wow! I can stay up now. Oh boy, this is some cramp. Must be the blood finally circulating freely through my veins, without any difficulty.

Just to be on the safe side, I'll turn facing the bed and hold on to the railings. If anything, I could always plunge face first onto the bed.

Wow! No need for that, I'm standing all right.

Straight as an arrow.

This feels bloody good!

I can feel my legs. Hurts like hell, but what a blissful pain. The kind of pain I prayed and longed for during the past five years.

Well, this is unexpected.

I am ready for the world again. I can go for walks, stop for a coffee or a stiff drink when I feel for it and I will not give a toss about the price.

Who knows, probably even Geraldine Joy would see me with different eyes now that I am on the mend. Ok, I'm probably deluding myself a bit now, but what the hell, dreaming is still free.

'Geraldine ... nurse ... somebody, come please!'

My voice was rather loud and clear.

So loud and clear it was, that in less than ten seconds or thereabouts, two nurses were in my room.

'Bernie!' yelled Geraldine all hysterical and nervous, pacing up and down my room like a headless chicken.

Then suddenly her tone changed. It was softer, more of disbelief and doubt, almost a whisper.

'My dear old man...' she said, holding my hand, 'oh my good Lord!'

There seemed to be a sense of relief in her expression. I was almost ecstatic.

'I have no idea what happened Geraldine, I just felt so different when I woke up...and I felt this...urge? I just felt light and there was no pain, and...' here I am babbling and unable to shut up.

'Oh my God!' she cries out, her African accent accentuated by her initial hysteria, 'Lorena, quickly call the doctor!'

Sister Lorena, the other nurse that came in with Geraldine Joy, was still pacing up and down my room, blubbering out something incomprehensible, flapping her hands. No surprise there, because this pleasant lady who is in her mid-fifties, is Italian, and we all know how loud and emotional these Mediterranean are.

I'm starting to get frightened. After all, I am in my early eighties, so all this commotion and excitement can be a bit too much.

Sister Lorena stomps out of the room while Geraldine Joy stays back and holds on to me.

'Ah Bernie,' she says, slightly calmer now, 'just try to relax my dear.'

'I don't know, I ...' I hesitate at first, 'what if I am unable to stand up again?' I suddenly notice, very much surprised at how my speech is flowing. I do also feel very light-headed.

'Does this mean I have recovered? Do you think I can go home again?' I blurt out, not really sure what questions to ask first.

'Dr Sewarajan is on his way. He won't be long my dear Bernie,' she replies a bit calmer now, while still holding on to me, her deep African accent ever more apparent. I try to make it to the armchair.

'Please, just hold on to me,' I am still rather insecure about my regained ability, 'you know, just in case my wobbly legs give in. You see, I haven't done this in years...'

'Don't worry my love, I'm beside you.'

Geraldine Joy is sweetness personified. She's originally from Zimbabwe but has lived in the UK for about 25 years. I know she has a lovely daughter who must be in her late teens because she has shown me her picture many times. I don't know if she is married or not, and quite honestly I prefer not to find out. That would only disappoint me. I prefer to secretly have that illusion and idealise her as I have since I first laid eyes on her.

Suddenly, she turns around, and her bottom looks more appetising.

We get to the armchair slowly but steadily, it's amazing how light I feel on my feet. Just as I am sitting down, Dr Sewarajan walks into the room, accompanied by Sister Lorena, who is now much calmer.

'Let's have a look,' says the doctor while taking my left hand gently, scrutinising me from top to bottom. Suddenly I feel a bit faint, but I hear him speak again, 'looks like you have been able to stand up... how do you feel, after the short walk you just took?'

'A bit tired, Doctor, but I felt no pain whatsoever and nice Miss Joy helped me.' I reply, still amazed at my clarity of speech.

'I do have to do a few tests,' the doctor continued very calmly, 'we have to check that all is in order, especially here upstairs,' he explains, tapping my temple, 'that is where the damage is done when one suffers a stroke.'

'I understand.' I try not to let this sudden change excite me too much lest I relapse and end up worse, both physically and emotionally.

The doctor instructs something to the nurses while he goes to fetch some equipment to carry out more tests. Or at least, that's what I think he meant.

What happened next occurred at too fast a pace for me to take it in. Dr Sewarajan entered and left the room numerous times, with charts, thermometers, stethoscopes, small devices that made weird noises; you name it, he brought it. Then later in the morning, another colleague came in. They discussed at length using words I had no idea existed and even less understood.

Finally, Dr Sewarajan announced to all that were present in the room:

'I must announce with some sadness on one hand, but with great relief nevertheless that our dear Bernie will be leaving us very soon.'

I heard him say something about my brain activity returning back to normal. It seems that certain cells had regenerated unexpectedly, those cells that allow the brain to send messages to my nerves, that in turn allow me to regain movement.

This felt like a dream.

I noticed Geraldine and Sister Lorena muffling up their cries, despite the stream of tears pouring down their cheeks. Mind you, I was getting a bit misty myself.

I was speechless, but thankfully, Geraldine Joy was doing all the necessary talking on my behalf. Well, she had been looking after me for some time so she knew what to say.

'We need to contact his son and daughter immediately Dr Sewarajan.'

Dr Sewarajan agreed and continued reading his charts.

I hoped they would react positively. I was, after all, their father.

'Doctor?' I asked with some apprehension, 'do you think I am fully recovered? Will I be able, despite my age, to lead a decent enough life until ... well, you know, until I, well, die properly?'

'On very rare occasions,' he replied laconically, 'these things are known to happen.'

'I must be honest though,' Dr Sewarajan continued, 'there is no guarantee there will be no relapse. Strokes are unpredictable little bastards. They are sly and silent. Just pray and hope for the best from here on.'

He came close and gave me a big hug. 'This is one of the rare occasions where I will be happy to see a patient go.'

The two doctors and Sister Lorena then left the room. Geraldine Joy stayed with me while I sat on the armchair, gazing at all the sights in my room.

I slowly stood up from the armchair, resting my hands on the armrest for balance. I gave the room a good once over as I slowly made my way back to my bed.

To my left was the hospital bed with its protective side railing. It was the most uncomfortable bastard of a bed, but I appreciate that in my circumstances, I hadn't much of a choice.

Next to it, on the very clinical and hospital like side table, stood a picture of my beloved Denise in her prime. A small lamp stood next to the picture, the weak yet warm light of it has been my night time companion on many a sleepless night.

A commode stood between the side table and the door. A cruel reminder of how dependent I had become of the kindness of the nursing staff.

To my right, a long dressing table, with hand-wash basin, my toiletries nicely and tidily stacked up. There they were, Brut my favourite aftershave lotion, Old Spice, the only cologne I ever used in my life, my toothbrush, toothpaste, brush, and shaving blade. Those little objects that were my usual grooming tools, but for the past five years, I had needed a helping hand to look presentable and dignified.

Finally, behind the armchair, under the windowsill, was a long table with some of the books I stopped reading years ago, once my concentration had weakened too much to retain a sentence, let alone a paragraph.

Also stacked very orderly, there were pictures of my two children, my two grandchildren, and a few of me in my prime – some on my own, others with Denise, and a couple of snaps with my children and me.

I continued my short walk towards the bed, noticing how easy it got with every step I took. I didn't even need any support from Geraldine Joy.

Suddenly, a scary thought came to me and I changed my mind.

'Geraldine, I am going back to the armchair,' I said nervously. 'What if I go back to that miserable old bed and I can't get up again?'

Geraldine Joy shook her head and laughed. 'Do whatever you feel comfortable with Bernie. If you like, just rest and take a little nap. I am sure all this commotion must have made you tired.'

I walked back to the armchair and sat down. I felt somewhat tired and dazed. I also realised I hadn't had any breakfast yet, with all the excitement going on, I forgot to be hungry.

I can't remember when I fell asleep, or anything thereafter. Can't even remember returning to my bed, but when I woke up, my son Geoffrey was in the room standing by the window. He was alone.

'Geoff, how long have you been standing there?' I ask, still with a sleepy and slightly droopy voice. 'You should have woken me.'

He turns towards me, a weak smile and glassy eyes greet

me. He looks drawn. 'It's ok dad. You seem so peaceful laying there,' he speaks quietly, probably forgetting I was already awake. 'I came across as soon as I could!'

'So what are we going to do? Am I to still stay here or can I go and stay with one of you?' I ask, then almost cursed myself for the second question.

'It's hard dad, no one was prepared for this,' Geoff replies and I notice he chooses his words carefully. 'Don't you worry dad,' he pauses and looks out the window, 'everything will work out just fine, it is just...well, it'll be hard to get used to.'

I shot him a jolting look when I heard the last bit. As if I wasn't aware of that. Five fucking years it's been! But he is right. They cannot risk me being far away from medical assistance if a sudden relapse or something worse happened.

I just fell asleep again.

I nearly went into a panic when I woke up, I couldn't recognise the room. Then I remembered.

This is Geoff's house.

I'm surprised with all these sudden changes, all this excitement, I still haven't had a heart attack. But it's good to come back to Geoff's home.

The room is decorated sparsely. I supposed they never expected me to recover and be a guest in their house, so I shouldn't complain. It is medium to small, off white walls with two plain shelves on one wall, stacked with a few magazines and maybe two or three old paperbacks; the ones you usually find in toilets or surgery receptions.

The bed is comfortable enough, single mattress, no railings and positioned against the wall opposite to the one with the two shelves. At the foot of the bed stands a narrow veneer wardrobe with three small drawers at the bottom. For the few possessions I have left, it is more than adequate. The wardrobe fits perfectly between the bed and the wall opposite. On that same wall, there is a medium sized double-sash window covered by a plain, pale, baby blue curtain that doesn't darken the room too much but leaves out enough light when required.

It's strange, but I cannot remember arriving here, yet I seem to have enough clarity of mind to take in all the details around me.

Strange, many of the events at the nursing home now seem very hazy to me. Of course, at my age, all this can be a lot to handle. I can't even remember, no matter how much I try, whether I said goodbye to the staff at the nursing home, especially my lovely Geraldine Joy. I would hate to come across as ungrateful after all they did for me. I should ask Geoff.

I walk to the window and draw the curtains. It is lovely and sunny outside. I can tell I'm on the ground floor because right before me lies the back garden with well-groomed grass, a few toys scattered about, a small decking area with a round green plastic table surrounded by four plastic chairs, its parasol closed and neatly tied up. I notice a small shed right at the very back of the garden as well.

Now, however, I am hungry and I could kill for a plate of toast and butter and some scrambled eggs. An English Breakfast Tea with a spot of milk and two sugars would also go down a treat!

Before though, there is a lot to unload. I can walk now with much more balance and relatively unaided, but I think I will have to buy myself a walking stick.

The guests' bathroom is small but has the basics. A very clean white porcelain hand-wash basin, the WC, and a very small shower that even Liam, my seven-year-old grandson, would struggle to fit inside.

While I wash my face with the warm water, I notice as I look in the mirror, how much I have aged. Well, I am eighty-two, so no surprise there.

Anyway, it is good to be able to hold your willie unaided while having a leak. Ah, the little pleasures of life…

When I went into the kitchen, Marie and Liam were already well into their breakfast.

'Hello!' yelled Liam, half of whatever cereal he had been

ANT RICHARDS

trying to chew spurting out in the process. Marie simply rolled her eyes in silent resignation at her son's newly created mess.

'Good morning sweetheart,' I replied and bent over to kiss his forehead, 'Good morning to you too Marie,' I turned towards my daughter in law.

'Hi there, I hope you slept well last night,' she said as she walked to the stove. I noticed they had a picture of me on the wall left of the stove which Marie straightened.

'Yeah, almost like a baby. Where is Geoff?'

'Geoff had to leave early for work. He has an early start you know.'

'Oh, ok.' I was a bit disappointed. I hadn't seen much of him since leaving the nursing home, or at least I couldn't recall having many conversations with him since. This short-term memory can be a pain at times...

'But don't worry; I'm sure he'll have more time for you tonight than he did yesterday. You know, he's still struggling to assimilate what's happened. In fairness, we all are.'

'I too am finding it hard to get used to Marie.'

No sooner had I said that she brought me a full plate of scrambled eggs and two slices of toast with a delicious layer of melted butter.

'I'll get your drink in a second.'

'You're such a sweetheart Marie,' I tucked into this decadently scrumptious feast of a breakfast, as I hadn't done in years.

By the time I finished, I was so full that I started feeling sleepy again.

There was, however, something I had to do as matter of urgency. I would check with Marie first though.

'Marie, are you very busy this morning?'

'I have to take this young man to school in a few minutes. Why, is there something you'd like to do?'

'Uhm, I just wanted to visit Denise's grave. I haven't done so in more than five years... well, you probably know why... it's such a lovely day, I –'

'Don't worry Bernie, my dear. I'll take Liam to school then

we'll be back for you. Don't go anywhere just yet.'

'Oh thank you! That'll give me time to get ready and all. We can buy some lovely flowers on our way there.'

She came over and kissed me on the forehead

I realised when I got back to my room that I hardly had any clothes. Most of what I had had been given away or something and all I had left was pyjamas, loose fitting trousers and open shirts, one or two cardigans and pretty much that was it.

I found a chequered shirt and a pair of beige Chinos. Because I hadn't done much walking in the past five years, I hadn't a pair of shoes to my name; a pair of house slippers and flip-flops were just about all the footwear I had left.

About half an hour later, Marie arrived. I heard her walking into the kitchen, drop a few things on the kitchen table, and heard her say something that didn't sound very coherent from where I was.

I suppose at my age, my hearing isn't as sharp as I'd wish. I decided to reply something anyway.

'Won't be too long Marie, I'm just combing my hair,' I replied back. Comb. Brush. I hadn't thought about that, nor did I have any idea where my comb or brush was. Still, I managed to straighten what little hair I had left and assumed it looked in order.

'Ok, I'm ready when you are my dear,' I announced.

Marie smiled back and started walking towards the side door that led to the garage. 'First, we'll go to the garden centre just down the road and buy some flowers,' she said as she fidgeted with her portable phone.

'Of course, but ... I,' I just remembered something very important.

'What is it?'

'Well, I ... I don't have any money on me, but –'

'Oh, no need to worry about that! For Christ sake!'

'No, no, I promise, as soon as my life gets back in order I'll repay you for this.'

'I said there's no need to worry about that…' She then put her phone inside her handbag.

I left it at that, but it suddenly occurred to me that I may become a heavy burden to them. I had no idea what happened to my finances after the stroke. Not that I was swimming in riches, but first the stroke, then being hospitalised and finally ending up at the nursing home, well, spending money didn't seem to be my main priority. Afterwards, I simply lost track of what I had, sometimes of who I was or where I was. Thinking I'd end my days at the nursing home, money was the last thing on my mind.

As she reversed to get on the main street, I suddenly remembered what it was like being in a car. I had stopped driving after I turned 72, mainly because I was unable to afford the insurance premiums for old farts like me. I did, however, enjoy going for a ride and having somebody else drive me around.

I felt like a young child going out for a spin, taking in everything that passed before my eyes. Hollyfield road, with its rows of neatly built semi-detached two-storey houses, most of them with well-trimmed and nicely decorated front gardens. I noticed the trees were much taller and fuller than they were when I last saw this street more than five years ago.

At the corner, we took a right onto Mill Lane High Street. On the left was Delford Park. A long stretch of open green space that made a lovely contrast with the overcrowded buildings pinned together on the right side of the road. These were littered with corner shops, cafés, Chinese and Indian takeaways, a chippie, Ross' hardware store – which I used to frequent a lot after retiring, more than anything for the company and an excuse to have a chat – the Tradewinds Pub, a William Hill outlet and many others.

Just in the middle of Mill Lane High Street, we arrived at the garden centre. We headed straight to the flowers department where I chose a lovely bunch of red carnations. These were the flowers I'd always bought for Denise's grave. Why change, I thought.

Marie continued driving until we reached the corner where Mill Lane turns into St. James' drive. Not long after, we reached the small driveway on the left that leads into the parish of St. James' Church. The gravel-stoned driveway ends at a small parking lot and right behind the small Church was the cemetery.

Unlike most cemeteries, this was an open expanse of well-groomed grass. From far, one could easily mistake it for a Country Club golf course. There were no tombstones identifying the graves. Instead, well-polished grey marble plaques identified each plot. I remember, before I fell ill, even on ugly, rainy days, one felt at ease visiting this cemetery. It gave the feeling of being in some sort of Memorial Park. Bright coloured flowers sprouted from the middle of the plaques, which had perfect round holes for that purpose, adding a multi colour mantle over the green expanse.

I still managed to remember the exact location of Denise's grave. Five years, rusty bones and a stroke hadn't denied that part of my memory.

For reasons I find hard to explain, I felt Denise very close to me. It could have been all that contained emotion, so many years longing to visit her grave, lay some flowers and have that silent conversation with her. The only time I could actually talk without her interrupting me or arguing...

Today, however, I felt as if she was beside me. I felt happy. Marie came over and put her hand on my shoulder as I sat contemplating Denise's plaque. She didn't say a word, but I sensed that she was happy as well.

Look my dear; can you believe it? I've recovered after all these years! I couldn't wait to come and see you.

But as much as I miss you, and God knows how much I have, I am not ready to leave just yet. See, I got a second lease of life!

Like everyone, I had made many mistakes in life, enough to cover for even my grandchildren's share of them.

This time it's going to be different. Before my mental faculties began to decline, I spent many a moment regretting all the things I failed to do, always finding a reason to justify myself.

And fat good that did for me!

Not this time. No. Never again.

We stayed there for quite some time and Marie, bless her heart, sat next to me, still making no sound and holding my hand. I suddenly looked towards her and I saw what looked like a trail of tears on her cheeks and slightly red puffy eyes. Strangely enough, I did not feel the urge to cry.

While driving back home, I felt as if a heavy load had been taken off my back. There was a sort of wellness inside me, which I found a bit hard to explain.

Ah, what a glorious day, a few puffs of clouds dotted the sky, the soft and warm sun gently stroking my face. It was definitely a good day to be alive.

I went into my room to change into something more comfortable. I was tired after this morning's excursion.

I took off my flops and socks, tucking these tidily inside the flops. Then, I laid back and rested my head on the pillow. As I closed my eyes, I started to conjure memories of past happy times in my head. I was slowly starting to remember stuff that happened before the stroke. Simple things really. Any event, situation, little milestone, however insignificant that brought back fond and happy memories. Things I had not remembered or thought of for a long time. They were all coming back, vivid, as a reminder of how beautiful life can really be.

To think that sometimes, I spent so much time making myself bitter over things of which I had no control.

My eyelids, however, were stronger than my will to stay awake and soon I fell asleep.

'Jesus Christ, what's all that racket going on?'

The clatter of cutlery, footsteps and distant voices rudely woke me up from my placid nap.

How nice, I hear Geoff's voice. And young Liam. They are home! I'll put on a pair of comfortable slippers and go outside to greet them.

Following the source of the noise, I arrive into the dining room.

Ok, thanks for calling me, I mumble beneath my breath.

To my surprise, everyone is sitting at the table; Marie and Liam on one side and Geoff at one end of the table. Everything is set – plates, cutlery, glasses, and dishes.

How strange, there is no place reserved for me. It is as if they aren't expecting me for lunch. Anyway, wasn't Geoff supposed to be working?

'Oh, you're having lunch now...' I casually remark to see if they react at all.

They don't.

Geoff just turns his head towards me and swallows whatever he is eating before replying.

'You were asleep so we thought you just wanted to rest.' He continues eating.

'Ah ok,' I reply somewhat taken aback.

'Liam!' Marie suddenly shouts, 'stop playing with your food. Hurry up and eat. You'll be in secondary school by the time you finish with this plate.'

I stand under the dining room's arch waiting for someone to ask me to join the table.

No one does.

'Well, I'll just go in my room.'

'Ok, fine,' both Marie and Geoff reply, and continue fussing over Liam.

Even Liam was too busy messing around with his food to take much notice of me. Suddenly I feel I am some distant, forgotten fixture in the house.

I walk out and head back into my room.

I thought my son, my own family, would have been happy to see me well and better.

Ok then, I get the drift. After all, what else can an elderly, decrepit eighty-two-year old, almost senile man, offer the world?

I might as well go back to that wretched old nursing home and waste away peacefully. At least over there, they feed and look after me.

And, there is Geraldine Joy.

But I don't really want to go back there. I have a family. Or don't I?

I feel like I want to cry.

Frighteningly, I am starting to feel that I am not getting used to my new recovered self, as strange as that may sound.

'I am going for a walk. I should be back for supper,'

Again, nobody replies.

Hmm, so it seems we're too busy to listen to this grumpy old git.

As I walk towards the door, I grabbed my cardigan and cap from the coat rack, open the front door, step out into a mild, sunny day and shut the door behind me. It's almost a quarter to five in the afternoon. There are a few kids walking about, some mums pushing their babies' buggies, and hardly any cars passing by.

For a change, the pavement is not littered with fallen leaves, traces of chocolate, chewing gum or sweets wraps or dog crap. At least I can walk without having to rely on a third eye I ain't got to avoid slipping and hurting myself.

A bruised heart is more than enough for me today!

But this walking thing is draining the life out of me. I may be stretching it a bit too far.

Of all the places in the world. How the hell did I get here? I never knew the address. I barely remembered Geoff's address, let alone here.

Christ, I'm knackered! It must have taken me around twenty-five minutes to get here.

God, this feels strange. Suppose it's that stupid voice inside me drawing me back.

To be honest, I have nothing against it or the staff. It's what it represents.

And I thought I had beaten the bloody old place.

But here I am now, standing at the main gate, catching my breath, longing to go back inside. I would even be grateful to get my same old room back if that were possible. Having Geraldine Joy nearby would be a bonus.

What's all that movement going on? And the ambulance?

Probably another old bastard about to bite the dust. Or maybe, already mingling in it.

I sometimes wonder if the Old Reaper is commission-based.

Let's go see who it is this time.

I pass through the revolving glass door reserved for visitors – after all, I am no longer a resident.

I am never in a hurry when it comes to finding out who is about to cross through the pearly gates, but curiosity can be a nagging bastard sometimes. I just hope my fate is not similar to the cat's one.

I follow the commotion and reached the block where everyone is assembled. I walked out into the mid-house patio, noticing how most of the geraniums were already in bloom in their thatched flower boxes. They looked beautiful.

Unfortunately, I have no time for contemplation.

There we are, Callaghan House. The house where I had been confined during my five-year residency.

Might as well go inside and look for my old room.

As I confidently make my way through, I notice the medics and nursing staff going about their business.

At the first turn in the main corridor, I hear some voices, a low hum at first. As I draw closer, the volume increases, albeit, only slightly.

I reach some nurses, but they seem to ignore me, probably too busy with whoever is deciding to die.

There is Sister Lorena. Her cheeks are red and her eyes a stream of tears.

I slow my pace as she approaches towards me.

'Sister Lorena, hi ... it's me, Bernie, you remember me don't you?' I am almost whispering as she draws closer me. She lifts her head, but she seems to look past me. Then, she suddenly bursts out in tears and continues walking towards the end of the corridor.

How very strange! She did not even say hi.

There is a small group of people outside one of the rooms.

Hang on, that's my room.

Ah! Geraldine Joy!

She is standing at the door. Her arse is unmistakeable! Although she has her back to me, I sense something is not quite right with her.

Well, there you bloody go!

It didn't take them long to get some new bastard in my room.

Anyway, whoever moved in didn't seem to last too long.

It'd be nice to have my room again if they readmit me, and now that I am mobile, it would be much easier. I could go out and spend afternoons on the patio, take strolls near the fountain, talk to the other oldies – the ones that ain't gone gaga yet.

I can barely make it to the door now. Damn it! I have to crank my neck to see inside.

Geoffrey?

Marie, Liam, they're here too. Oh my God, even Laura... *and* Celine.

But whom are they visiting?

Hang on a second! Didn't I leave Geoff and his lot having lunch at home not even half an hour ago? How did they get here so fast, and who's that lying in what used to be my bed?

Oh, there's Dr Amir Sewarajan.

Oh, shit...

Throughout the years, I've become very much aware of the mortality of those around me. Denise, for example, gone almost fifteen years, many of my lifelong friends who have died off over the years. It is the natural order of life I guess.

The logical outcome.

There he lays; fragile, old, and in a way, alone. I suppose, when you are going through the process of dying, whichever way it happens, you are on your own.

It all makes sense now. Talk about an anticlimax.

I can be such a delusional fool at times. In the end, it was all a load of bollocks!

It was a nice little adventure. It felt good while it lasted.

Am I disappointed? Well, yes and no. It's accepting the shit that's hard. I suppose it's just a matter of time now.

I guess this gives me that bit of time to put things in perspective.

Shit! Dying can be complicated. It's as bad as filling out those damn tax returns. I now understand what they mean about the only two things certain in this world.

Right, there is no point standing here like a ghost seeing my dear ones suffer – I'll have enough time for that very shortly.

My body is tired, battered; it is beyond repair. Now that I think of it, the past five years I had been living on borrowed time.

The old brain, on the other hand, is still pretty sharp, and that's how I want to go.

It's got to be good beyond the point of no return. I've been no saint, that is a fact, but I have lived well and done my share of good, and I am sure that will count at the final weigh in.

I made my way towards the bed, looking left and right, glancing at everything in my room for the last time.

Yes, after all, it was still my room. This wish, I did get in the end.

I looked at myself lying serenely on my bed. My breathing was very slow, yet uniform. My face looked rested, almost peaceful even. I was even wearing my favourite pyjamas.

My eyes suddenly started to feel heavy and I drifted inwardly without much resistance. I felt a violent but very brief shudder. Then suddenly, all pain and discomfort, as I had sadly grown to know the last five years returned. I felt the all too familiar cramps in my limbs once again. However, despite all the pain and discomfort, I felt a sense of relief.

Geraldine Joy came closer and leant over me. I weakly tried to open my eyes, to no avail. Everything felt too heavy.

'Bernie, sweetheart, can you hear me?' she whispered to me. I vaguely recognised a sad expression instead of the cheerful smile and giggly laugh that always warmed my heart and I think still triggered that weird but pleasant reaction in me, lower down. This time, however, there was no pleasant reaction. Lower down or anywhere for that matter. I contorted a weak smile and she held my hand, squeezing it gently and calling Geoffrey along.

He came over, so did Marie and little Liam. I was barely able to make out their faces but I felt their presence. I believe I gave them a weak smile; however, I felt sadness in their faces. Geoffrey said something I was not able to understand, but it sounded sweet and comforting. At the same time, I could almost swear I heard Liam saying 'I love you, grandpa'.

Those was the last coherent words I heard. My eyes finally surrendered. I could still hear sounds in the room although they too were becoming distant. They were soft murmurs that blended confusingly, only this time I seemed to understand each and every word clearly.

My eyes were shut, yet I felt no darkness. Slowly and pleasantly, fear, confusion, and anxiety turned into serenity, bliss, and peace.

The people in the room, however, were still talking.

Just let go, darling, there's no need to fight it anymore.'

I recognised the voice.

'You've had enough my love...'

The voice I loved and missed so much.

'...just let go...'

And that is exactly what I did.

The Full Circle

Maybe I'm not crying, maybe I don't mind
But it hurts just knowing that your children won't be mine
'Nobody knows' Mike & the Mechanics

There it is. Mel was petrified the second she recognised the room number. There was also that niggling sense of excitement and curiosity.

The door had been left slightly ajar. On purpose maybe?

Excitement had turned into nervous expectation; heart-thumping anxiety had now become full-blown panic. She had come this far – a dangerous, impulsive, and why not, life-changing decision. There was no turning back now.

This is stupid. Absolutely crazy. Mel was terrified.

With trembling hands, she straightened her skirt, she didn't really need to but did so nevertheless. She tossed her golden wavy hair behind her shoulder and pulled down her blouse a bit, again another unnecessary exercise. Small droplets of sweat were appearing under her eyes, above her cheekbone, which she gently wiped off with her right hand as her left hand nervously pushed the door open.

At the end of the room, Matt, tumbler in hand, stood looking out the oversized window. The lights in the room were dimmed to a bare minimum, the spotlights' filaments barely glowing, while the crimson and gold of the dying day poured into the room. His loose white linen shirt like a canvas for the different shades of the dying sun, while he stood statuesquely looking out towards Victoria harbour.

Outside the window, the skyscrapers donned in their neon frocks prepared for their nightly serenade of light. In Kowloon, on the other side of the harbour, the ICC tower rose imposingly, ready to lead the multicolour display.

Standing under the doorframe, Mel focused on the tumbler Matt was holding. Glenfiddich was her guess. She still remembered that to be his malt of choice. She stole a glimpse or two at the room.

Nothing seemed out of place – a few sheets of paper and a book neatly arranged on top of the night table turned work-desk. A light cream jacket hung behind the chair. A pair of loafers at the foot of the queen sized bed. Yes, he was still as tidy and organised as she remembered him.

Mel took another shy step forward.

Then another.

Matt dared not turn around. He simply swallowed hard and stared out the window.

Mel finally took a deep breath and resolutely walked towards the window. She stopped dead behind him and took another deep breath. She nervously stretched out her right hand but stopped just before reaching his shoulder.

Matt still didn't move.

'I've come here dozens of times and I never cease to be amazed,' Matt finally spoke. 'There is something about Hong Kong I find so fascinating,' he said flatly.

'The organised chaos, the smells, the speed on which people seem to live and at the same time, the serenity they display in all this rush.'

Mel just stood in silence behind him, not really taking in what Matt was saying. Her breathing had become faster.

'Please come and stand next to me, I promise I won't bite.'

Mel timidly walked up to Matt's right side and stood in front of the window. She hardly cared about the view, Hong Kong's magnificent skyline, or anything beyond the window, no matter how spectacular it was. Unlike him, however, she was still unable to utter a word.

She of all people.

Mel had always been the more talkative of the two.

'Is that the best you can come up with Matt?' she finally spoke. 'I was expecting the killer line to blow me off my feet,' her raspy drawl sounding as nervous as it felt sexy.

'Maybe I'm nervous,' he replied with a nervous sigh. There was an uncomfortable pause. 'Anyway, after all these years, I thought we were beyond *impressing* each other.'

'Charming!' Mel replied softly, stifling a giggle. More relaxed, she finally let out a tight smile.

In the mid-eighties, Matthew Hogarth's mother, a successful lawyer in a banking firm in London, relocated to

Boston after accepting a very attractive position at an investment firm. His father was a famous session guitarist. He had played with high profile artists in the UK as well as Canada, the USA and recorded in many renowned studios across Europe. Moving to Boston only meant a longer commute to wherever he needed to perform.

Melissa Appleton, born and bred in Boston, came from a relatively well to do conservative Catholic family in Massachusetts. That meant going to good schools, a large family home in the suburbs of Boston as well as a smart city pad on Berkeley St between Newbury Street and Commonwealth Avenue. Later, she became a Graphic designer, obtaining her degree at Massachusetts College of Arts and Design.

They met in late spring 1997 at a library where Mel worked part-time, three days a week. Matt, 27 at the time, was doing some research for his thesis in Business Studies and visited the library to request a particular title to work on. Mel, a month short of her 24th birthday, happened to be on duty that day.

Matt immediately fell for her deep aquamarine eyes, her electric blond streaks against a luscious forest of brown mane. Her voice was soft and raspy yet had a very sweet tone to it. Her well-proportioned lips always quick to draw a childish pout when necessary enhanced her slightly freckled cheekbones on a porcelain-like pale white facial complexion.

Her figure was not that bad either; at 5'1 she had all the right curves in all the right place, with the odd extra here and there, but that just made her more credible – a sophisticated yet sweet and provincial East Coast beauty.

It was her sweet and innocent smile however, that captivated Matt. That goofy smile, as he used to tease her, that caught his eyes the first time they met; the smile that would melt his heart every time thereafter, for any stupid reason, or no reason at all. The wretched goofy smile he realised would never greet him when he woke up every morning.

Mel fell for his witty and dry sense of humour. Matt could be sometimes clumsy with his words yet always tender with his actions. She found his manners refined and loved his natural laid-back charm despite all the stereotyping that Britons carry in the United States. Being relatively tall and lanky, he carried a slight athletic build. He had light brown eyes and deep black wavy and usually untidy hair, tamed with a makeshift ponytail.

After that first encounter where she so efficiently helped Matt out with his enquiry, he mysteriously found excuses to go back to the library. After the third visit, he plucked up the courage to ask her out.

Matt was already eight months into a relationship while Mel was also seeing someone; a strange relationship according to her as it seemed her boyfriend spent more time with his football, beer-guzzling buddies instead of her.

Ironically, Mel seemed to have everything Matt never sought in any woman he had ever dated or even laid eyes on.

Despite her very sophisticated upbringing, Mel possessed a provincial sweetness and a warm, engaging personality. That, together with her aquamarine eyes was reasons enough to turn Matt head over heels.

Their first date was at The Baseball Tavern, near Fenway Park on Boylston Street. In between cocktails, Matt impressed Mel with his stories of holidays in Europe as a child as well as life in his native Lee, in South East London up until his family relocating to Massachusetts. Wanting to impress even further, he also mentioned meeting some very famous and interesting musicians through his father's job.

Matt was, in a way, some kind of exotic creature to her.

Meanwhile, Mel's furthest expedition had been to the Virginias to the South and Milwaukee to the west. She dreamed of someday visiting far-flung places like Paris, Rome, Athens, London and even Lee, based on Matt's description of his hometown!

After leaving the bar, and while inside the lift on their way down, Matt kissed Melissa for the first time. Totally unexpected, Melissa was however by no means offended and it took all of a microsecond for her to correspond, much to the nervous looks of the others sharing the lift.

They left the building hand in hand and walked towards Matt's car; Mel blushing and Matt feeling like a million dollars.

'This is my beauty,' Matt announced, proud as they reached to where he had parked his car.

Mel was impressed at the sight, mainly for the wrong reasons. The car, a '82 Ford Fiesta, had certainly seen better days. With a few small dents here and there, a few minor scratches and signs of rust around the wheels, it resembled its owner; juvenile, rough on the edges, with a European flair to it, defiant, rebellious, yet cute and loveable.

Matt opened the passenger door for Mel and invited her in.

'So Mel, what do you think, the pinnacle of class and sophistication, eh?'

'Reminds me of you,' she replied all giggly.

'It's all I can afford at the moment,' he had replied embarrassed.

Immediately, Mel pushed up the lock under the window and made as if she was about to open the door and get out of the car.

'What are you doing?' Matt feared his battered, little, un-American car had scared her off.

'You see, I'm not sure whether I'm supposed to ride in the car or help you push it.'

They looked at each other, Matt with an incredulous expression and Mel just stifling her laugh.

Matt leant over and turned her face towards him: 'You asked for it.'

This time, the kiss was more prolonged and passionate.

Inevitably, a few days later, Matt and Agnes broke up. There was no animosity; in fact, all things considered, it ended quite amicably.

Melissa literally dumped her boyfriend who didn't seem very aware or much affected by the breakup. He probably treasured having more time to drink, watch football, and hang out with his buddies.

Two months into their relationship, a new position as Chief

Graphic designer at a magazine in Buffalo, NY became available. Struggling to get a decent job in Boston, this was too good an offer for Mel to refuse. Matt, on the other hand, was established as a Junior Accounts Assistant at Chartered American.

He had no issues with Mel going to Buffalo and was more than happy to see Mel's professional opportunities grow. They were young, just starting in their respective careers and this was just a progression in their lives. Besides, Buffalo was not that far away.

Not that long after, Matt's mother was made redundant and after a few months looking around struggled to find a new job. Both she and his father returned to Britain within six months. Even back home, finding a job proved a challenge for her, even at positions below her professional level.

Meanwhile, Matt continued progressing in his job and both he and Mel alternated visiting each other.

Just before the end of 1998, Matt's mother suffered a heart attack. He rushed back to the UK to be by her side and spent the next three months commuting between Boston and Southeast London. As her condition deteriorated and fearing the worst outcome, he eventually quit his job and returned to the UK.

Melissa's career was skyrocketing. In fact, she accepted a higher position at the same magazine's head office. In New York. The distance finally took its toll and not surprisingly, their relationship slowly withered away, if not their feelings for each other.

Finally settled in the UK, Matt joined an advertising firm. During one of his commutes to Boston, he and Agnes unexpectedly rekindled their romance, and she made plans to join him by the end of that year.

On his last trip to Boston, in October 1999 Matt and Mel saw each other for the last time. This last trip to Boston was the final process of Agnes's relocation to the UK.

Matt, however, was willing to throw all that away if Melissa decided to join him in the UK. Even at the expense of dumping Agnes for the second time.

For the same woman.

A long shot he knew, but then, he and Mel never fell out of love. One thing he was not willing to negotiate was returning to the USA. He wanted to be close to his mother during what he suspected, were to be her last days.

He spent three weeks in the USA liaising with the UK Consulate in Boston, finalising all the legal paperwork. In between, on a wing and a prayer, Matt took a few days to go down to New York to make his final gamble.

Matt arrived at New York's Penn Station and checked into a modest guesthouse in Little Italy.

Later that evening, they agreed to meet for a drink and a talk at a diner on Lexington.

Amongst many other things, Mel told Matt about this new person she was seeing and how things seemed to be going from strength to strength between them.

That did it. Matt did not ask the question. Painful to hear how well things were working between them and with all that was going on in his life, a gracious rejection from Mel was probably the last thing he needed. He decided to cut his losses, take the money and run, so to speak.

After all, things were going very well between him and Agnes. His mother's poor health aside, he was finally getting the professional break he deserved in England.

What Matt failed to notice was that Mel was dying for him to ask her to go with him: to London, Afghanistan, Mars, the bottom of the ocean even. That was what she was hoping Matt's side-trip was all about.

Lars, the landscape engineer she was dating, and who in the space of nine months, would eventually become her husband and the father of her two children, the man she would still be married to eleven years later, would always be a second best substitute for Matt.

In the end, there were goodbyes, best wishes, and no plans for the future.

Agnes joined Matt just before Christmas that year and they eventually married in August 2000. Two offspring, Michaela and Julian, resulted from their union.

Matt's current project for the Advertising Company he worked for, involved the opening of a branch in Hong Kong. He had already travelled there at least five times that year.

He was recruiting graphic designers to help with the creation of the new offices and magazine formats for this particular branch in South East Asia. The new offices were going to be located on Connaught Road in Central, on Hong Kong Island.

One Melissa Henderson applied for a position. She had been working as a freelancer for the past two years.

Although Henderson was her married surname, Matt recognised it and thought it had to be more than a coincidence. Graphic Designer, living in Boston – she had moved back about three years after Matt returned to the UK. The US is a big country, but the chances of two people with the same name, living in the same city doing the same kind of work were one parallelism too many.

Matt finally turned round to face her.

Time had definitely altered her but not to the extent you would expect. He laid the tumbler, which was less than half an inch full, on the floor.

As he rose, he slowly studied her. The skirt hugged her waist and thighs with a jealous grip. Her figure was not far from what he remembered when he last saw her. He felt tempted to put his hand around her waist but thought better of it.

At least for the time being.

Her face had aged as one would expect after twelve years, but her features had not changed much. At 37, her beauty had turned more elegant, sublime, and sensual, unlike the fresh, youthful cuteness he fell in love with thirteen years ago.

Age, however, and time, in this case, had been kind to her.

Her aquamarine eyes were still stunning, shockingly beautiful but lacked that juvenile spark of earlier years. They now oozed a more tender, mature, and sophisticated shine to them.

When he finally levelled face to face with Mel, he simply stared at her. Melissa noticed his receding black hair now harboured a healthy population of greys by the temple and scattered about on the rest of his head. The salt and pepper addition making him appear more distinguished.

As expected, he had also aged slightly. He wore what looked like a two-day stubble, which gave a rough edge to his features; a kind of edge that Melissa found rather attractive. His eyes though still had that deep penetrating gaze of his youth.

'What have you done to your years Mel?' he asked quietly, staring deeply into her eyes. 'You look so gorgeous.'

'See what you've been missing Matt?' she replied. She placed her two index fingers on his chin, rubbing against the stubble and reaching for his lower lip. 'You look pretty hot yourself.'

She winked and offered the sweetest pout.

Matt was one of those men that grew more handsome as they got older. Long gone was the wavy hair and ponytail. She could still see traces of the piercing in his left lobe from where many years ago a small silver loop used to hang, proud and defiant. He had to let it go once he started working for Chartered American. That was the last bastion of rebellion that he had to shed once he settled in the smartly suited and high-flying workforce of the banking world.

'You've missed your fair share of me as well.' He bent down and took another sip of his tipple. He rested the tumbler on the floor again and stood up, again facing Melissa.

'Do you really have to interview me tomorrow?'

'Well, you have travelled half the bloody globe for this wretched position, you know,' he replied, without much emotion in his response.

'And... not sure if you noticed, but I *am* the Project Manager. I will be interviewing all the applicants. And yes, I do want you to apply for this job.'

'Regardless of... *now*?'

Neither Melissa nor Matthew had an answer to that.

'Will tonight have any consequences to our interview?' Mel asked softly but still nervously.

'Apart from the obvious embarrassment between us... I can't think of anything really.'

'Matt,' she held both his hands in hers. 'Are you happy?'

'Are *you* Mel?' he asked blankly, staring into her bright blue eyes.

'I asked you first.'

He got close to her and gently kissed her lips. Melissa did not pull back. She did not reciprocate either. He gave her lips another peck, waiting for a reaction. Still, there was none.

Matt pulled back and turned towards the window. *What an idiot...*

Night had already fallen over Hong Kong. Scores of light boats, tugboats, Star Ferries, and all sort of small vessels zigzagged across the harbour in no particular direction or order. Matt's feelings and emotions were just as chaotic.

'Why did you stop?' asked Mel, still standing in the same spot.

'Why did you not continue?' A slight irritation betrayed his flat response.

'Matt, honey,' she whispered carefully choosing her words, 'where did it all go so wrong?'

'I guess we just gave up too easily.'

Something had to happen sooner or later, she thought. The timing seemed right. They were still relatively young and still found each other attractive.

Matt knew, deep inside, he was still madly in love with Mel. Like any kind of disease or virus that lies dormant in a body, all that's needed is a trigger to unleash the symptoms. Love is no different.

Matt laughed nervously and said, 'do you remember the first time I kissed you in the lift at that bar in Boston?

'Of course, I remember, our first ever kiss.'

Mel smiled slightly embarrassed as she remembered that night.

Back then, she was unable to react so Matt had to do all the hard work at the time.

This time, however, he was scared this kiss would evolve into something irreversible.

She laughed, 'maybe we should go out and try kissing in the elevator.' She turned and walked away.

Matt turned around and just stared as she walked the length of his room towards the door.

'Well, don't just stand there like a zombie?' she said from across the room as she held the door that led to the hallway, a mischievous glint piercing from her eyes.

'What the hell are you doing woman?'

'I'm going to the hallway, *duh!* Maybe I only react when you kiss me in elevators.'

Matt weighed his options. Should he run and see who gets to the lift first?

Childish!

Shut his room door and simply let it die?

Foolish.

Or just bite the bullet, pull her in, shut the door behind her and let fate and destiny take its course?

Too late, she was halfway across the corridor.

Matt walked to the door, still barefoot. He hesitated for a moment, looking left and right across the corridor, while still holding the door. Suddenly, he saw a head pop out from behind a wall.

'Hurry up Matt!' she said in a loud whisper, 'I don't have all night!'

That sexy, raspy voice was too much to resist.

...and she used to call me childish!

He started to walk, but after five or six steps, he picked up and ran. Mel did not move; she stood against the column with her back to the twin lifts, nervous and curious.

Matt stopped just inches from Mel.

The Baseball Tavern, Boston 1997. All over again.

Matt met Mel's eyes. He had longed for this moment for so many years. Life certainly knows how to deal a bittersweet hand.

He felt around Mel's still curvaceous hips and pulled her towards him, their lips just inches apart. Their breathing merged into one pattern and their heartbeats drummed in unison like a well-choreographed rhythm section.

They looked into each other, unsure who was to take the first step. Their reflection into each other's eyes was as eternal as that inextinguishable flame that kept their dormant passion alive.

'You know what Mel?' Matt finally whispered to Mel.

'What is it, babe?' she whispered back, in the sexiest and most velvety voice possible.

'Call the bloody lift!'

They somehow stumbled into the first lift that arrived without really caring as to whether there was anyone inside. It was empty. Not that they noticed it straight away. Not that it really mattered.

They clutched each other's hands. Matt got closer to Mel, lips millimetres away now.

No sooner had their lips made contact, burying them in a savage kiss than the doors closed sealing them inside their new temporary cocoon. However, there was no movement. Neither of them had bothered to press any floor button. There was no need to go anywhere. They had everything they needed inside that lift.

Their hands fell motionless to their sides, the only thing holding them together were their lips locked in a passionate kiss that held twelve years of waiting. It was obvious there was much catching up to do. Despite this, they felt like two strangers kissing for the first time and that felt great.

Mel stood motionless leaving it down to Matt to guide her,

as his lips travelled across her face. There they stayed, recognising each other once again, the concept of time thrown down the shaft.

But they were different.

Mel no longer wore the same French perfume that always reminded Matt of her. The same fragrance he would try every time he passed through the women's perfume department in any major store, just to remember her.

Matt felt different. His kiss wasn't as urgent as it was back in Boston. It felt passionate, yes, but composed, confident.

Finally, there was a reaction. With both their eyes softly shut, Matt became bolder. His lips continued travelling across her face, like a blind man recognising his way through touch.

Then the bell rang. The lift stopped with a gentle jolt. Matt and Mel were still kissing, but they slowly became aware that their private world had come to an abrupt pause.

The doors opened, and two German businessmen entered the lift and pressed their floor, while very excitedly commenting on something, in German of course, which neither Matt or Mel spoke nor understood.

They all alighted on the same floor. The Germans left first, and not too far behind Matt and Mel followed, like two hormonally overcharged teenagers giggling at their little mischief.

As soon as Matt and Mel reached his room door, they resumed their kissing, too desperate to wait and get inside. The Germans continued to walk ahead and finally stopped at one door at the very end of the corridor.

Mel was slightly wary of the Germans, but Matt's kiss was far more interesting.

After a few seconds though, Mel separated from Matt's lips.

'You know, I think I should go back to my hotel, it's getting quite late now,' making not much effort to walk towards the lifts.

Matt just frowned and gave a slight nod.

'Yeah, right,' he replied sarcastically while he sifted through his pockets, finally produced his key-card and opened the door to his room. Very gently but with firm determination, he took her hand, and silently guided her into his room.

They didn't even bother checking on the Germans.

Once inside the room, their kissing became more intense and urgent. As far as they were concerned, the world was as good as ending that very night, so every second counted.

Without turning on the lights, they ended up on Matt's queen-sized bed, clothes were strewn across the floor in their wake.

Those same hands that many years ago wandered unscrupulously and unashamedly across their bodies remembered every move as if only a few days had passed since they last touched each other. It was those same warm shivering hands that Mel loved and longed so much, that nostalgically caressed her without any predetermined route.

The confusing scent of Mel's perfume, Matt's cologne, blended with their perspiring bodies and the unique scent of Oriental laundry.

'I love the way you look at me,' Mel managed to whisper between kisses.

'And I love the way you say it,' Matt replied almost as breathless.

That is what Matt loved so much about Mel; her capacity to transport them to somewhere else within the confines of where they were, with just one kiss, just one caress, or simply looking into his eyes.

Between the lavender-scented cotton sheets, with the dim lights, and the wide window that timidly showered their room with the city lights of Hong Kong, they made love for the first time in almost thirteen years. Like two adolescents exploring each other for the first time, the double-glazing windows drowned the outside hum of the city, camouflaging their socially illicit but emotionally necessary rendezvous.

Exhilarating, pulsating, electric spasms invaded their bodies, as each thrust from Matt sent Mel into hysterical arrests. If this was what heart attacks felt like, she thought, she was prepared to die a thousand deaths.

They had finally arrived in their own parallel world. A world that only belonged to Matt and Mel, where they were free to love without rules or any trace of guilt.

This was probably the last chance they had in their lifetime. They had seized it, but more importantly, they had finally closed the circle.

After making love, they talked at length, about anything and everything, more like two long lost friends than lovers. Then they made love again. Talked again, made love again, losing count of how many times they made love and stopped to talk that night. Not that it mattered, but just for the record.

The hazy sunlight made its lazy appearance over North Point, casting a golden, orange layer over Victoria Harbour.

Matt and Mel welcomed the new day with a lazy but just as rewarding love making session as daylight shyly bathed the room. They hadn't bothered to draw the curtains. After kissing every inch of her body good morning, and she reciprocating just as tenderly, Matt got out of bed and headed to the window.

He looked out and just gazed at the impressive skyline before him. Now he loved this city even more.

Mel finally got up and started retracing the trail of clothes left behind when they entered the room. She placed them tidily on top of the bed and joined Matt at the window. Matt just stared at her.

Matt leant over her and kissed her gently on her shoulder.

'You know what honey...you and I never danced,' she tossed back her hair and kissed Matt gently on his lower lip.

Matt just looked at her and gave a half-smile. He so loved that raspy voice of hers.

'We never really went clubbing, did we?'

'We had our songs though...,' Mel got closer and softly kissed Matt on his chin, slowly making her way up until their lips met. 'The ones that told our story.'

Matt buried his hand in her hair as their faces rubbed against each other's, while Mel's hands worked their way around his back.

Suddenly, Matt separated and gave her a quizzical look.

'Hey, what slot do you have today?'

'Come again?'

'The interview babe, what slot were you allocated?'

'Shit! I think I was in the 9.30 am slot,' she suddenly realised in a panic, all the magic of just a few moments ago evaporated into thin air. 'I can't turn up in these clothes...'

'What clothes? You're naked.' Matt teased her.

'... I need to shower, I –'

'That's ok, I won't use that against you,' Matt joked trying to ease her panic. 'Look, it's still early, you'll be fine,' he reassured her, 'just get a cab, go back to the hotel, and meet me at the office. See? It's just turned 6.35, you've got heaps of time...'

Mel nodded nervously and hastily ran into the bathroom clutching her clothes. Matt just stood leaning against the centre beam of the windows, watching as she scurried away.

He suddenly stopped smiling, thinking of the day he had ahead at the office.

Two minutes later, Mel came out of the bathroom, fully dressed, lips glossed, hair properly shaped, glowing glint restored in her eyes. She looked ridiculously beautiful.

'Bloody hell, you look gorgeous.'

'Gotta go, Matt,' Mel ignored the compliment, 'I... well, just...'

'Leave it, honey. Just get your stuff together for the interview and ... make sure you don't get your knickers in a twist.'

She looked back still puzzled and searching for words.

'Asshole!' she finally blurted out and made for the door.

'Mel.'

Mel made for the door as she straightened her skirt and tossed her hair.

'I love you.'

She didn't reply. She just looked at Matt, nervously twitched her lips, turned around, and left the room.

There was still a whiff of perfume left in her wake that Matt tried hard to breathe in; a desperate attempt to retain those last moments with Mel. Furthermore, the sweet aftertaste of Mel's kiss still lingered on his lips.

Matt turned and walked to his bed. He sat down and stared blankly at nothing in particular. He turned and grabbed her pillow pressing it against his face. It still smelled of her. He only then realised how knackered he was.

He also realised how much he already missed Mel.

Mel hurried to the lifts and in her nervousness pressed both the 'up' and 'down' buttons. Fortunately, the lift that arrived was a 'down' lift. She got in, nodded a good morning at two Chinese ladies who were already inside. The button was already pressed for 'G'.

Her eyes suddenly got misty and not long after, a single tear trickled down her cheek.

I love you too, you idiot!

Matt was already on his third heavily loaded coffee. His first of four interviews for that day was about to start.

For him, it was a matter of routine and going through the motions; he already knew who was going to get the job. It was hard to resist the temptation of having her close by, of occasionally repeating what happened the night before again, and again.

Mr Günter Moller from Nuremberg, Germany knocked on the door; he was the first interviewee.

Next, came the turn of one Glenda McQueen from Dunedin, New Zealand.

At 9.26 am, Matt called the receptionist and asked her to hold back Mrs Henderson. He needed another coffee, as well as another freshen up before he took her on. His eyelids were as heavy as a concrete pillow.

The receptionist replied there was no one else waiting. The

9.30 interviewee had not turned up.

This was unusual of Mel. How would he justify hiring her if she cannot even turn up on time for the interview? Matt decided to wait a few minutes before calling her direct.

9.35. Still nothing.

He nervously paced up and down his office.

At 9.40, he grabbed his mobile from the desk and called her, when suddenly the buzzer on his desk went off.

The taxi journey from Matt's hotel took all of seven minutes and by seven am Mel was already in her room.

After she arrived, she decided to call Cathay Pacific to find out if she could catch the earlier flight to Tokyo instead of the 18.45 she was already booked on. It made more sense to arrive earlier in the afternoon than close to midnight.

More importantly, it made even better sense not to attend the interview. Coming to Hong Kong knowing that Matt was her potential interviewer was bad enough. Spending the night with him had been total madness. Working alongside with him would be emotional suicide.

Cathay Pacific confirmed a seat on the 12.35 flight to Tokyo-Narita at no extra cost. She rebooked on that earlier flight. All she had to do was revalidate her ticket at the airport. She barely had an hour to refresh and leave the hotel.

Before that though, she took out her Iphone and emailed a quick message to the company explaining she had a family emergency and would have to forgo the interview. She apologised profusely and thanked them for short-listing her for the position.

As she sat on her bed, she drew out her passport from her handbag. Looking at the bio-page, she stared at the line that contained her married surname: Henderson.

She loved the name and all it represented, but could not help thinking what it would be like to have Hogarth in its place instead.

She closed her eyes and softly bit her lower lip as she felt a solitary tear make its way down her cheek.

Matt's last words to her still resonated in her head as a sweet curse and a bitter blessing at the same time.

I love you too, you idiot!

HE CLIMBED OUT THROUGH THE BATHROOM WINDOW

No clock beside my bed, don't try to wake me
No phone upon my wall, who's going to call?
No knock upon my door, no news to shake me
Nights like the one before, I can't take no more

Beaujolais – Alan Parsons Project

Solitude is a bitch of a companion.

Especially at one in the morning. Alone. In bed. Lying, or should I say, prostrated on a single, soggy mattress, springs piercing through your vertebrae and ribcage, cancelling any possibility of rest. Unless of course, you knock yourself unconscious with half a bottle of whisky, six Valium pills or a well-connected hammer just under your cerebellum.

The constant, torturous ticking of that small, useless clock nailed on the wall opposite me, hardly helps. Meanwhile, my guts rehearse an off-key concerto of internal combustion, the occasional fart adding a less colourful note to my predicament.

Priceless.

It feels as if this day refuses to draw its final curtain, although it technically ended just under an hour ago.

And I'm only on day three of our ten-day holiday in Carranza.

How I love this place, though. It's sleepy main plaza, gently bathed by the Mediterranean sun tamed with balmy easterly winds flanked by even lazier jacarandas passed their brief blooming period provide the idyllic setting for a leisurely stroll after a quiet morning at one of its quaint coves. At any corner, small family owned bars guarded by the protective shadow of the main *Iglesia de la Santa Providencia* church welcome locals as well as the few fortunate tourists that happen upon this town for their aperitif or any excuse for a cold, teeth-gnashing beer.

But my love affair with this coastal village on the south eastern Spanish coast almost ended last summer when we decided to tag along with my brother and his odiously unpleasant wife. The fact that I still have a brother and even more surprising that he still has a fully functioning wife is only proof that God exists. Although sometimes I feel He doesn't necessarily play for my team.

Lou and I were not necessarily close, but we just about got along in general. The day he married, some three years ago, we started to get on less well. Nevertheless, there was still some element of 'well' in our relation.

Simply put, my brother's wife is evil. Diabolical. Rather than being born, she was brewed in some witch's cauldron!

My predicament this year, besides this clock from hell and the torture-friendly mattress smuggled out of a dictator-run fourth world country's prison is much worse.

My in-laws.

Obviously, I did not learn from past errors. They too are a pair of cauldron-spewed elements from hell. The icing on the cake? My two teenage kids; hormones maxed beyond humanly tolerable – moody, obnoxious, and put politely, pain in the arses to be around at the moment.

Yeah, I was a teenager and a pretty bloody wild little piece of shit I was as well. So maybe it's payback time, whatever...

I sometimes wish I could take a sabbatical from life until they turn twenty-one, but I'm not sure the missus would take kindly to that idea.

I still love them, though. And my wife.

Not so my in-laws. Nor my sister-in-law.

I still cannot sleep and the more I am able to not sleep, the more pissed off I am becoming.

Annoyingly, everyone else is fast asleep – I can even hear the in-laws snoring away.

Of course, my wife, not content with inviting her parents, also bequeathed them with the nicest suite in the two-bedroom villa we rented for the ten-day stay. They are her parents after all.

Just to make things worse, earlier today, the bastards, who have contributed to fuck all during this holiday still had the guile to order a takeaway seafood platter – I am allergic to shellfish. And who paid for it all?

I rest my case.

At least I take comfort knowing that my two moody teenagers also hate them.

Unfortunately, my wife, whom I love to bits, is still their daughter.

Perhaps, the only upside to my holiday dramas is *Bar El Galeón*. A faithful refuge during good and bad times, the small, unpretentious tavern sits on the eastern fringe of the village's main square. The drinks are good and cheap; tapas are varied and ingenious. The service, however, is slow, lazy, sloppy, and unpredictable.

But there is Silvia.

Silvia must be in her early twenties, with white skin naturally tanned by the soft Mediterranean sun. Big brown eyes flanked by perfectly groomed brows adorn a lively, terse golden face. Her well-built frame with perfectly contoured curves affords a view that is hard to look away from; the turquoise waist-hugging dress she wore today conjuring images and desires puritans would love to censor. Her long black, wavy hair flowing untamed and rebellious simply invites trouble.

The only source of enjoyment and escape from the poisonous tentacles of my evil sister-in-law and everything that blemished last year's holiday, I made *Bar El Galeón* my new holiday 'local'.

This year, with the in-laws in tow, has been no different. It was a relief to discover Silvia still worked at *El Galeón*.

She even addresses me as *Mi giri favorito* – the cheek-in-tongue term Spaniards use to refer to Brits – something like *My Favourite Englander*.

Earlier today, I learnt that the bar's owner is Silvia's godfather and she just finished university, however, she had become yet another victim of Spain's economic crisis as jobs in her line were very scarce.

Now that we're better acquainted, I have been tempted to ask her if she has a boyfriend, but that could only open a dangerous can of worms, whatever her response.

Moreover, one year into my forties, what would a lovely twenty-something want with an almost old fart like me?

There is also Óscar, a pleasant local in his early fifties who lived in England for almost fifteen years. He returned to Spain seven years ago after discovering his wife was having an affair with one of his Spanish students. In their home. On their bed. A no-brainer.

He confessed it might have been a blessing in disguise. She never wanted children and he was desperate for offspring and with his biological clock ticking northwards, he was running out of time.

No sooner had he returned to Spain, than he met Carmen; single, mid-thirties, ok to the eye and actually quite pleasant – in his own words. They married; she bore him two boys within three years. A done deal.

A private English teacher and the main cosmopolitan figure of the village, Óscar is a bit of a celebrity in his own right. He can also drink any bastard under the table!

Great! I have now made one of the worst mistakes any insomniac can make. I looked at the clock. It has just passed 1:42 am, and I haven't felt more awake in my life.

And now, I need to go for a piss.

Ah, that's much better!

I watch out the window, strategically fitted opposite the toilet. A clear starry sky providing natural moonlight into my bathroom.

Well, that's about it.

And yes, I have washed my hands.

As I slowly walk towards the bathroom window, a wicked, mischievous idea invades me.

No, come on, not me, not at my age.

This is immature and childish, but not a bad idea.

It could get *really* embarrassing if I get caught.

Well, one still has needs.

My hands tremble. My nether region is palpitating in anticipation.

What the fuck, I'm up for it. Once won't hurt. Anyway, I need some sort of release.

Good thing the hinges are well greased on these windows.

I just have to remember the shrubs outside, so must be careful not to make noise!

Ok, here we go!

Unlike The Beatles' version, this I'll do in reverse, and by no means protected by a silver spoon.

This light cashmere sweater was a good idea.

Ok, so let's see... It is a fifteen-minute walk into the village.

I've never been out this late in Carranza but I'm sure there must be some bar that's still open. A quick drink and back home, I do need some release, but I'm taking no chances.

The B road that runs from our chalet is poorly lit, but at least it's not all that lonely; houses every thirty or so yards dot about left and right of it.

There we go!

The main street. Next right and ... another fifty yards or so I am in the main plaza. Not bad at all!

Hmm, the plaza seems lit, not only that, I can hear some voices as well. There is life in the village centre. Hopefully, it is friendly life as well.

As I walk confidently towards the plaza, a voice suddenly stops me in my tracks.

Fucking great! Just what I need; roadside bandits! Shit! I am such an arsehole.

'Hey, you are the giri!' says a youthful male-sounding voice in Spanish.

Ok, calm down. Don't do anything rash...yet.

On the other side of the one-way street, two young men cross towards where I am. 'Yes, it is the giri!'

'Que pasa chavales!' (*What's up guys?*) I reply somehow apprehensively.

'Hombre! What are you doing on your own so late? The wife kicked you out?' says one of the men. I recognize him. I have seen him a couple of times at the bar.

'Venga hombre! Que no te vamos a hacer nada!' he suddenly laughs noticing my fear. *Come on man! We're not going to hurt you!*

'Hey, we've seen you a few times at *El Galeón*, I am Juanjo,' says the older looking man who can't be more than twenty-five, 'this is my friend, Antonio.'

I am still a bit apprehensive, but try not to show.

'I couldn't sleep and I really need a drink,' I reply more confidently.

'You've come to the right place, giri!' the second man says.

'Are any of the bars open at this late hour?'

'Come on!' says the younger looking chap, 'this isn't Madrid or Barcelona. By eleven o'clock, everything is dead around here,' he explains shrugging his shoulders. 'But come with us to the plaza, we have a little party going on. Even old Óscar is there.'

As we walk towards the plaza, I can already sense the festive mood. My two newfound friends start calling out names: 'Carlos! Pepe! Que pasa chavales!' (*Carlos! Pepe! What's up guys!)*

From the distance, I distinguish a number of silhouettes lazily assembled.

What I presume are both Carlos and Pepe stand up from the foot of the statue of some local saint, or celebrated figure. They walk radar less towards us.

'But look who is here!'

I recognize the voice. It's not only the English nature of the sentence but also the person who speaks it. It is Óscar, the village's celebrity extraordinaire.

'So, my giri friend, what are you doing here amongst these ruffians and lowlifes?'

'Well, not having the best of holidays, and tonight I... well just needed a break, really,' I reply unashamedly and quite surprised.

More surprisingly, I feel no ounce of remorse. 'So, how do giris like me get a drink around here?' I demand festively.

Óscar summons one of the boys. 'Make yourself useful! Get this fine man a drink. He is my guest of honour tonight.'

About an hour later or two drinks after, whatever came first, we decided to move on.

Amazingly, I can still remember the names of those assembled at the plaza. Yours truly, of course, Juanjo and Antonio, the two young chaps that rescued me from my aimless walk down the main road. Then there is old Óscar, Carlos, Pepe, and also among the group are Encarna, a sultry brunette probably in her late twenties, and Magdalena who seems to be having it with Pepe, or is it Juanjo? Óscar doesn't seem to be faring too bad either. A fine and curvaceous chick called Leticia seems to be oozing all over him. The lucky bastard.

'My dear English brother in struggle,' Óscar very solemnly announces, 'as my very special guest and in honour of all the years we have known each other,' he adds, although to be fair, we had only just met last year, 'I will take you to a very exclusive drinking club. Only select people are allowed in, I must add.'

'I am most honoured my learned friend,' I reply, just as solemnly, albeit drunk and slurry. That *garrafón* we were drinking was not only as big as a barrel; it was pretty lethal as well. With its blend of port, brandy, and maybe aniseed, the high it gave me was of biblical proportions.

'What is so exclusive about this place if you don't mind me asking?'

'It is illegal,' Juanjo whispers in slurred English.

'Then it has to be damn good,' I reply in equally befuddled Spanish.

'You see,' Óscar starts explaining the history of what seems to be the only speakeasy in the village, 'those of us with a cosmopolitan background require that our select and discerning tastes be catered for appropriately in the outback of Spain's province.'

The group listens in awe, silently priding themselves to be part of this select Masonic type brotherhood.

Óscar comes up to me and pulling me aside he whispers, 'I devised this plan, my friend. This fucking town can be so boring at times and family life can just drive you mad...'

A visionary. Crazy as fuck, deranged maybe, but a visionary

nevertheless.

'Now my dear comrades, time to go,' he quietly announces.

Suddenly, a silent, complicit edge starts to build around the group.

We quietly start picking up all the cups, bottles and other bits and pieces scattered about the plaza. In the meantime, Óscar makes a quick call on his mobile phone.

As we start walking, I steal a quick glance at the statue of the famous town figure serenely and sternly witnessing our little soiree.

We walk past the main church, which occupies the north side of the plaza in its entirety. Quietly, we go around it and suddenly stop at the back of the building. Óscar then takes a couple of reticent steps forward and quietly knocks at a rugged looking wooden door.

A few seconds later, it slowly creaks open and a hand timidly appears, handing something to Óscar. He checks the item, gives an approving nod and the hand disappears the same way it slid out only seconds ago. Immediately after, the door creaks itself closed.

'Comrades, we are ready,' Óscar announces softly.

I follow the rest of the group's cue. We walk through a narrow alleyway behind the church until we reach another door.

Óscar puts the mystery object in a keyhole.

So, it was a key.

The door opens soundlessly. Óscar ushers the group in. I am the last to enter.

Once we are all safely inside, he shuts the door behind him. It is a dimly lit room, walls bare bar a small window, wooden shutters concealing the outside world. Besides the door that let us in from the street, another smaller door on the opposite wall are the only features in this room. No furniture. A well enough maintained wooden floor contrast with the dirty off white of the walls.

'Now Mr ... Danny,' Óscar suddenly stops, 'I know your name but not so your family name.'

'McVie.'

'Danny McVie,' he repeats, 'see guys, I bet you never heard such a smart-sounding name in your lives before.'

They all look at me silently.

'Mr Danny McVie,' Óscar continues with what sounds like an initiation ritual, 'I have shared many drinks with you in *El Galeón* whenever you grace our town with your presence. You seem a pleasant enough person, and I even find a sort of kindred spirit in you,' he continues in remarkably good English. 'Your unexpected presence in the plaza was a divine signal and it just made me think, "here is a man who will appreciate our very unique society" so I thought...'

Oh shit. Is this some sort of satanic cult? I'll probably be gang raped and quartered, my remains thrown in the lake, or offered to some pagan god or something.

'I thought,' he said after gathering his breath, 'this giri will be a great drinking companion for our select group. Therefore, Danny McVie, I welcome you to our exclusive brotherhood.'

'Well, I am truly grateful Óscar, but why the secrecy if you don't mind me asking?'

'Carranza is a very traditional and conservative village,' Óscar explains, 'therefore, very boring and backwards. Some of us have lived in big cities, I have even travelled as far as London.'

'That is why,' he continued, 'I created this place. We could have done something different, but people were too comfortable, too complacent, and not very adventurous.' He puts a hand on my shoulder, 'so, together with a few other colleagues, we thought, "let's create something bordering the clandestine", something to give us a certain... edge! A speakeasy... that is what you call it in English, right? Here we drink, smoke, laugh, debate, and interact with like-minded comrades, no *Health and Safety* bullshit. Here, we are free from the ligatures of conventional moral constraints.'

'Seems fair,' I agreed.

I was enamouring myself to the idea.

'Well, it's time to go through,' he announces.

Óscar put the same key through the other door's keyhole. Once the door was open, he ushered our group through. Again, I was the last to walk through the mystery door.

'Welcome to *El Lar de Utopia*.' (Utopia's liar).

We walked down a short flight of steps before levelling onto a dimly lit landing about eight to ten-foot long by six-foot wide. Old looking, cream coloured wallpaper with fine green stripes adorned the walls. Again, at the end of the landing, another dark oak door stood between us and the promise of clandestine pleasures.

Óscar gave three knocks on the door. A few seconds later, the door opened inward. We immediately walked in with swaggered but very dignified steps.

Only once in my life have I been to a speakeasy, and that was in Paris. Like this one in cosmopolitan Carranza, one had to follow a ritual to gain entrance. Once inside, the atmosphere was relaxed, jovial, and obviously had the touch of mystery, prohibition, and intrigue that these premises usually offer.

This place, however, immediately exuded something untoward about it. There was definitely an air of secrecy, a whiff of darkness, illegality, together with a relaxed sense of bonhomie amongst the guests. In addition, I could feel an air of hedonistic abandon throughout the place.

I was slowly beginning to warm up to it.

The room itself was rather large. Classically decorated, it held three large sofas, some armchairs and maybe four or five tables all in good repair that could sit up to four people around them. One large chandelier hung from the middle of the ceiling, in addition to individual standing lamps placed next to each sofa. This allowed for decent lighting yet still leaving a level of soft intimacy.

In addition to the door we entered through, there were two others in the room. At the opposite end of where we entered, there was a long L-shaped bar which occupied most of the length of that wall, only interrupted by the second door in the room. A large floor to ceiling mirror, shelves stacked with different bottles complemented the area.

Besides our group, there were more people inside the room. Soft bluesy background music provided a relaxed atmosphere to the room. I saw no waiting staff so I assumed one got drinks directly at the bar. *Hotel California* somehow came to mind.

'Well, make yourself comfortable my friend,' Óscar said to me as I took in the surroundings. 'I take it you have seen the bar area. We have pretty much anything and everything here. Even cigars!'

I thanked him and slowly walked towards the bar. After all, that was the main idea of climbing out the bathroom window.

I scanned the room and some faces I could not recognize. Others, however, became suddenly familiar. Amazing, how such small towns sometimes hold their fair share of secrets.

There was one of the street cleaners, who I've seen since my first visit to Carranza. A middle-aged gentleman who frequents *El Galeón*, and a young woman who works the tills at one of the village's convenient stores. She was perched on one of the sofas, legs entangled with those of a bearded young man, a bottle of red wine with two half-filled glasses on the small table in front of them. The image clearly spoke for itself.

They were engrossed in serious 'vocal' and 'manual' conversation, however, despite the obvious lustful intentions, they looked anything but raunchy, illicit, and embarrassing to a third person's eye, quite the contrary. They could not seem more at ease in these surroundings.

Just a few feet away on one of the larger tables, three men probably in their forties or so, were discussing the upcoming Spanish football season. In less than ten seconds, I discovered that one of them was a Barcelona supporter, the other a Real Madrid fan and the third man vociferously praised the virtues of Atlético de Madrid. Again, despite their passionate debate, no blood was being spilt; in fact, their body language revealed a more sedate, almost literary-like discussion. Spooky.

Not too far away, two elegantly dressed elderly men, tumblers in hand, were quietly conversing away. Very much relaxed and at ease, they were probably escaping their respective nagging better halves. Or maybe not.

Lastly, two women in their thirties and an older man played a game of cards, a bottle of brandy in the middle of their table and an ashtray with three cigarillos slowly burning away. Health and Safety gone with the wind.

I finally reached the bar where two barmaids were busy preparing drinks, their back to the bar. Already sedated by the tranquil atmosphere, I patiently waited to place my order.

I took a close look at what was on offer. Contrary to my first impression when I entered the room, the shelves didn't seem to offer great variety. The mirrors behind and the spotlights reflected on the shelves just gave the illusion of plenty.

I started to think about what would be happening back at the chalet. Would the family still be sound asleep? I couldn't spend too long in here. This had to be a swift one, a two rounder at most. The last thing I need is to incur the wrath of Mrs McVie.

'What can I get you, gentleman?'

'Ah, can I have a –' I replied in my almost good Spanish before my jaw dropped.

'What are *you* doing here?'

'Precisely my question *mi giri*,' Silvia replied in English, probably just as perplexed.

'You also part of this secret society?'

'We call it more like a...' she replied in a lower voice, '... how can I say... a members' club? I think that is a better description,' she clarified in her sexy Spanish accent.

'Members' Club...'

'Ok, it is a bit of a secret. But you know what small towns are like, too much old lady's gossip and boring village life.'

I could see her point, however, if this sleepy village had a fair share of forward-thinking inhabitants anyway, why not have this in the open? Although, come to think of it, in a town of maybe, what, eight/nine hundred inhabitants, twenty so-called cosmopolitans hardly made up a significant movement.

Point taken.

'I see our friend Óscar is quietly creating a cultural revolution in Carranza.'

'How do you mean Danny?' Silvia looked surprised as she wiped the same wine glass she'd been wiping since coming to take my order.

'Well, he created this little after-hours bar and found all these like-minded people, and...'

'And you believe him?' she nodded her head and gave a muffled laugh as she rolled her eyes up.

'This bar was my idea.'

'Look, Óscar is a bit of a character. He is a lovely man, but he fantasizes too much. His mouth is bigger than his brains. Whatever he tells you, you should multiply it by two and divide it into five. That much would be the actual truth.'

Again, point taken.

'So, what are you having my dear girl?'

'What do you recommend?'

'Are you here, erm, legally?'

I took a deep breath and briefly explained what made me climb out the bathroom window, and how I ended up here.

'Well, that is an adventure! I can see why Óscar added you to the secret society of Carranza's select drunks,' Silvia said with a mischievous giggle. 'I was actually looking forward to seeing you away from *El Galeón* sometime.'

Talk about building up a climax!

Man, she looked gorgeous. Her wavy black hair was tamed into a single pigtail, revealing a fuller face that simply increased her beauty. Tight waist-hugging grey denim simply beckoned mischief. A loose-fitting charcoal grey blouse concealing nothing but a laced black bra completed her night shift attire.

'This is an absinthe cocktail. My creation,' she winked her right eye at me as she handed the chilled martini glass filled with a viscose green concoction, 'I hope you like it.'

'How much?'

'On the house,' her fingernails naughtily stroking my fingers as she handed me the cocktail. 'Sometimes, money doesn't necessarily buy happiness. Cheers.'

As I studied my drink and digested her response, she leaned towards me, a pink cocktail in hand.

'Erm, cheers to you too,' I said as our glasses softly touched.

'I guess you won't be seeing the sunrise with us then.'

'Sadly not,' I timidly admitted.

Silvia smiled then pouted softly. 'That means we'll have to make tonight worthwhile.'

Lounged on a sofa, my face was inches away from Silvia's, my right hand around her lower waist, my left hand softly caressing her right fingers. I had no idea how and when I got there and made no attempts in finding out either.

I reached for Silvia's lips. She reciprocated without hesitation.

Money certainly can't always buy happiness, but Absinthe cocktails are the perfect substitute.

Without sounding romantic, corny, or pathetic, I felt myself floating as Silvia and I kissed. It was a very sedate, slow, and timeless kiss. Absinthe cocktails have that power, it seems.

My right hand almost numbed by the awkward position it was in, but not complaining at all, insisted in exploring new territories. Meanwhile, my mind was making exploratory enquiries on what would follow.

Silvia's hand gently explored my chest and expertly made its way south of my navel. Eventually, and with no shortage of relief, my right, almost comatose hand found freedom underneath Silvia's loosely fitted cotton blouse. Her back felt tender and soft as I gently climbed up her shoulders. Not at all mortified by the hurdle that her bra presented, I clumsily tried unfastening it.

When reality returned for a brief moment, I noticed that those left in the room simply got along with their own business. The football punters continued their civilized yet passionate debate. The young cashier and the bearded man were still engaged in manual and vocal communication. One of the elegant elders was nowhere to be seen, however, the other one was drinking amiably in the company of Juanjo and Pepe.

Even Óscar was already deep in conversation with the other barmaid.

'Wow Danny, the cocktail really loosened you up,' Silvia whispered.

'Did it?'

'I loved the poetic way you told me I had the nicest ass in town...'

'I did?'

'I was wondering how soon you would make some kind of move since you came back to Carranza last week.'

'You were?'

My incredulity just seemed to increase exponentially as I sank further into this Absinthe induced stupor.

'Of course! I've noticed the way you look at me at the bar and ... well, all those regular visits?'

'I never thought you could be interested? You are ... well, much younger than me, and I'm well –'

'You're married, so what?' she finished the sentence, 'anyway... what harm can a little adventure do me?' Then with a mischievous wink, she added, 'or you?'

True, especially in a place like this...

'Relax my lovely giri,' she pouted and got closer again, within kissing distance, 'this will stay between you and me.'

'And the other fifteen or so inside this joint,' I added slightly alarmed.

'What goes on in here, stays in here,' she reassured me.

Who was I to disagree?

'Look, I need to go back to the bar,' she said separating from our embrace, 'I shouldn't overdo my break, even if I am the boss. In half an hour, I'll walk through that green door,' she pointed towards the solitary door on the right-hand wall of the room, 'you follow me in.'

She noticed my confused expression as I looked towards the little green door and chuckled. 'Hey, that is just my office, where we do the takings, admin, etc. It's not what you are thinking. I don't own a ... how do you say in English, a *puticlub*?'

'Brothel?'

'Ah, yes, brothel ...' she clarified for my benefit. 'But, tonight I need someone experienced to teach me a thing or two,' she gave me a peck on the lips then swiftly returned behind the bar.

Just then, Óscar, whose image had somehow fallen off the pedestal I had previously put him on, approached me. He had about him a very slow, almost swagger-like walk. His burgundy cords, brown suede shoes, blue and mustardy checked shirt, and Paisley designed satin handkerchief ungallantly tied around his neck exuded the charms of a *'has been'* seventies heartthrob. The poor excuse of a David Niven-like moustache did little or nothing to help his outlandish look.

'So, how do you find the ambience in here my dear Danny?'

'It sure is a nice place Óscar, well done on you,' I didn't think it very prudent to confront him. For all I knew, Silvia could be lying as well.

'You see, my friend, we just have to inject a touch of sophistication, glamour, edge, and panache to this god-forsaken town,' he added while swirling his almost empty tumbler. 'If it weren't for this place, I swear *tío;* this town would not be worth living in.'

'Tell me something, does your missus know about these ... escapades?'

Óscar looked at me, giving a wry smile, took a deep breath then slowly placed a small cigar between his lips, drawing slowly.

After a few seconds, he turned his head to the left and blew out.

'Let me tell you this Danny,' he began, 'after my marriage went down the toilet back in England, I was left with a serious dilemma. I can't exit this world without leaving my mark, my legacy,' he explained with statesmanlike solemnity.

'I am a very traditional man. Nevertheless, I was reaching the point where if I waited too long, instead of kids, I would end up having grandchildren. I met Carmen here in Carranza. I wooed her with my stories of travels, adventure,' I could see the fantasist Silvia was talking about, '...and of course, my innate charm played a big role in sweeping her off her feet.'

Unfortunately, I had no choice but to listen to his diatribe. The effect of that magical Absinthe cocktail was worryingly wearing off, boringly sobering me again, and making it harder to assimilate the bull crap I had to hear.

'...so we reached a very convenient agreement. I married her, wiping off the stigma of spinsterhood.'

Man! This Óscar had a way with words!

'I grace this world with my rightful descendants, and everyone is happy.'

Fortunately, Juanjo turned up. 'Hey, Mr giri! You enjoying?'

'Er, yes, great place,' I replied, soberer than I cared to feel.

'Guys, I must say goodbye,' he announced, 'I have a lovely woman waiting for me and I can't make her wait.'

'Good man,' I reply, 'best get going then, go and do us proud Juanjo,' I say, bidding him farewell in the process.

Óscar pats Juanjo on the back as he ushers him towards the door, smiling approvingly.

'That *chaval* is such a devil,' he nodded proudly, 'very soon he will surpass his mentor in the fine art of seduction...'

My God, give me a break...

After coercing Óscar to invite me for another drink, and listening to his exploits for another ten minutes, Silvia waves at me from the bar.

'Erm, sorry Óscar,' I try to cut short our one-way conversation, visibly relieved, 'Silvia is calling me over to the bar.'

'Go, young man,' he replies, 'do not keep the dame waiting. She is hungry for love.'

Silvia mumbled something to the other barmaid, took off her apron, and grabbed a square bottle half-filled with a green liquid I suspect must be the Absinthe from the bar. How the fuck I'm supposed to make it home afterwards in one piece is anyone's guess.

With a discreet nod, Silvia ushers me towards the door.

I silently follow her inside, eager to discover what other *takings* take place inside the *office*.

The room is actually quite small. I start wondering how they managed to fit in the large desk that occupies most of the room. More worryingly, I start thinking where are we going to, well, sit? Lie?

'So,' I ask the wretched question, 'what do we do here?'

'Maybe help me with the accounts...'

Well, for every stupid question...

Here I am now. Seconds away from paradise. It is really happening.

No more fantasising about Silvia. Carpe Diem.

Again, the lack of space returns to mind but I won't even embarrass the moment asking another stupid question.

Silvia suddenly pulls me towards her and grabbing my hair, locks her lips against mine.

I now have her bra unzipped after slipping my hand behind her blouse. For the second time tonight.

We separate long enough so she can pull off the bothersome blouse retaking where we had left merely three seconds ago.

As we kiss, she expertly started to unbutton my shirt and my inhibitions.

Once our bare chests meet, the feel of her firm nipples against mine triggers my hands to squeeze her ass unashamedly.

She savagely caressed my back, while I continue exploring south of her rear border, savouring every movement, enjoying every inch I could get my hands on. With less finesse, she finally reciprocates on mine.

As most of my body became more sensitive to her touch, a certain renegade and rogue element started looking for trouble.

At the same time, my mind begins to wander in the wrong direction – or is it the right one?

Yes, that ugly, sometimes elusive, but mostly untimely gremlin called guilt slowly makes its annoying appearance.

If I am so cross with my in-laws, why do I have to betray Mrs McVie with a one-night-stand, albeit a steamy, sexy, beautiful one-night-stand?

Oh crap! What do I do? No one has to know. Just a quickie. In, out, yeah, ooh, nice, bang, wow! There.

Shit! How will I look at my family after tonight? Come on, what goes on in here, stays in here, and all that. Hotel California. Secret Brotherhood.

This is insane. I gotta stop! This is a once in a lifetime chance.

Fuck, what if I can't get out of here? No, this is not guilt taking over me. It is fear. Sheer, abject fear. I now realize I'm terrified at all this.

It was that bloody bed's fault. That chamber of torture disguised as a bed.

Maybe it *is* guilt, disguised as fear.

It could well be a nightmare. That's it. No. It better not be. We all know nightmares are not a good thing.

By the time I come back to myself, I mean, not the guilty self but the horny, cheat-to-be, I now notice I'm only wearing my underwear and Silvia is down to sin-inducing red-satin knickers.

Oh man, let's get it over and done with.

Fuck no, I can't.

'What's the matter, Danny?'

'I don't know... I...'

I really didn't know.

She took a small step back and sat on the edge of her desk. 'You are scared.'

'I... I just don't think I can go ahead with this,' I finally conceded.

'Yeah, I understand,' Silvia seemed sympathetic to my stupid predicament.

'I'm sorry Silvia,' I said looking away from her. I couldn't bear to see that beautiful woman, almost naked before me, ready to immerse herself unto me, only to be shunned away by a sudden burst of decency.

'Don't worry, I won't hate you for that,' she came over, lifted my chin and gave me a prolonged and sweet kiss. 'But if you change your mind, I'll be waiting for you. I really like you girl.'

As if there *would* be another chance.

We both got dressed in silence, the muffled noise outside the only thing breaking our awkward silence.

'Look, it's no big deal,' she tried to reassure me, 'it just shows you are a good man.'

That is just the consolation I need.

'Let's go out and get you a drink. On the house.'

Outside, the atmosphere was still jovial, although I noticed a few people had already left.

I finished my drink and started to make my way out. I walked to the bar and waited for Silvia to finish serving a punter.

'I think I must make a move. I have to make sure I can slip inside the chalet before anyone wakes up.'

'It will be fine Danny. It's only four in the morning. Just be careful you don't fall asleep on your way home. You don't want to read in the newspapers, *a girl found on the street asleep and drunk.*'

'Do I look drunk?' I asked a bit worried.

'You don't look it,' she said, looking at me with studious eyes, 'but three Absinthe cocktails and hormones at full speed...'

More like unused hormones...

Apart from a slightly dented pride, suppressed libido and a

guilty conscience from hell, I felt rather ok.

'Well, thanks for tonight anyway,' I painfully bid farewell to Silvia. 'I guess I'll be seeing you at *El Galeón*.'

'I hope so, Danny. And don't worry. Remember what I said to you before; what goes on in here stays in here.'

And what doesn't as well, I guess.

She blew me a kiss and continued to wipe some glasses.

I turned and looked around but Óscar had left. The rest of our arriving party were already engaged in their own rendezvous – happy, unaffected, unattached, no ounce of guilt in their faces. Like it should be in a place like this.

El Lar de Utopia; a fitting name indeed.

An underground haven where nothing is wrong and anything can be right. There are no laws, therefore, no rules can be broken.

And I thought I was open-minded. Until of course, I had the forbidden fruit before me and I chose to err on the side of safety.

As I walked up the steps, the air smelled damp and stuffy. I reached the top of the stairs and opened the other door. I entered the room that led out to the street. Contrary to when we arrived, the room suddenly seemed cold, lonely, and sad. It no longer had the sense of adventure I felt when I arrived with Óscar and his cohorts.

Maybe it was always like that.

Probably Óscar, his cohorts, Silvia, and the remaining members of that secret fraternity don't have that feeling of expectation every time they visit the place. To them, going there and enjoying the freedom it affords, is a foregone conclusion.

I looked around the empty room looking for answers. Answers to questions I couldn't even find.

I finally closed the door behind me, silencing the soft murmur from downstairs, and thus, shutting the door to the closest I came to freedom for a long time.

Well, I've finally found a question. In fact, two or even three.

Should I have stayed and finished the job? Could I live with myself after? Could I still look my wife in the eye and tell her I love her, that she is still the love of my life...despite her parents?

Could I still be the perfect role model for my kids?

Maybe what happens down there really stays down there, but what about in my head? Unless that cocktail was some sort of magical elixir that wipes out memories, I would certainly have remembered.

As it is, I still can't get over Silvia. Her touch. Her perfume. Her kisses.

Oh, shit! Let's get out of here before I go mad.

The cold of night is biting hard.

Fortunately, I had the good sense of putting on a cardigan, and even luckier, I didn't forget it inside Silvia's *office*.

Silently and carefully, I walk towards the side street that feeds from the main plaza.

The town is ghostly silent. Well, it would be at four something in the morning, wouldn't it?

Still, I mustn't draw any unwanted attention.

I border the main town's plaza; the same place where a few hours earlier I joined an orderly group of village partygoers commandeered by Óscar, the unofficial debaucher in chief of Carranza.

The main plaza cleared, I hit the town's main street where Juanjo and Antonio rescued me from my solitary walk to nowhere, only to introduce me to a night of gallivanting, debauchery that left me, well, nowhere actually.

Just as I turn to join the solitary B road that leads to my holiday chalet and the promise of more holiday frustration, two cats that either have the stingiest owners in town or are the unluckiest hunting bastards in the world lazily cross my path.

They both look at me indifferently, very un-catlike for these most untrusting of creatures. One of them opens its mouth as if it were about to meow, but has second thoughts and simply continues its walk. Its partner follows and soon they both disappear through one of the houses at the corner where the B road branches out from the main street.

Out of habit I suppose, I look both sides, but I am sure a car hasn't passed this corner for at least six hours. I cross towards the right side of the street; the same side where the chalet is.

As I make the tortuous walk up the road, I hear some stepping on the dry grass. It's amazing what one can hear in the dead of night. Other than the chirping of the odd grasshopper or the rustling of the dry leaves lifted by the lazy nightly breeze, there is an eerie silence about.

It can't be those two lazy cats, these steps sound much heavier, human even.

Also, very human is the sound of giggling coming from the same direction. I stay where I am, shielded by a slightly battered red Seat Cordoba. I crouch on the side of the pavement. That sound definitely comes from the opposite side of the street.

There they are! It is a couple, and they sound quite merry. They are too far away to distinguish from my concealed position.

Crap! I am only about thirty yards from home and safety!

They are whispering between them but the female is definitely giggling.

Ok... I'm gonna lift my head a little ... but it's difficult to see through two sets of car windows, and there's not much light either. I'll crouch down again and think my next move.

I'll have to wait until they walk away.

They are still standing on the other side of the road, still whispering.

Great! I also need to piss. As if things were not shitty enough right now.

This wait is killing me, not to mention my bladder.

Ok, they seem to agree on something. What it is, I have no idea, but at least they are moving.

Let's see if I can catch a glimpse of the couple.

Damn it, that woman doesn't stop giggling.

Fuck! it's Juanjo.

And that... must be the dame he was supposed to offer unlimited doses of love and lust. Good for him. At least he got lucky tonight.

Let's check her out.

Shit, no...

My heart sinks.

Fuck me, fuck me ten thousand times!

Silvia...

Why did I not stay with her? Crap timing to grow a conscience, I guess.

Huh, who would have thought?

There they are, these two – giggling, kissing, hands exploring their bodies radarless but with a damn good sense of purpose.

I'd never seen her smile like that before.

Yep, I'd never seen Mrs McVie so happy in such a long time.

THE SENTENCE

I take a pride in probing all your secret moves
My tearless retina takes pictures that can prove

Electric eye – Judas Priest

Running naked, splashing the warm foam of the recently crashed wave on the sand on a sunny summer morning is priceless. Accidentally stepping on a hole, you could have sworn wasn't there and falling face first on the sand is, well, stupid. But that's the way it ends. All the time.

Jimmy Kerr's eyelids feel heavy, dry, and grainy. Nevertheless, he still makes the effort. As his eyes adjust to the dimly lit room, he sadly realises nothing has changed. Same dream. Same ending. Repeatedly and ruthlessly cruel.

Has another day passed?

Just an hour?

He couldn't care less. There is no way of knowing, so why bother?

He just about remembers that one day – or was it night, again, the concept of time completely lost to him – he woke up naked and curled up into a corner of this white padded cell. Walls, floor, ceiling, everything is padded. Three dim bulbs arranged across the ceiling provide the only source of light. Again, these are switched on and off at different times and intervals making it hard for him to keep track of time.

Windowless, the only known connection to the outside world a small trap-door, from which his food bowl and latrine are dragged in and out at irregular and confusing intervals.

A loaf of brown bread, a slice of tomato, a piece of apple or pear, maybe a slab of cheese or wafer-thin slice of ham and a plastic cup of water is his diet; barely nourishing, but keeps him alive.

Jimmy's hair is now long, sticky, itchy, and straw-like. A long and untidy beard also furnishes his face. His lean and once steel-like arms are now saggy, pale, and flaky, not to mention the smell.

And the itching.

He has scratched so hard that he's ended up drawing blood and peeling the skin off. The scabs etched throughout his body are a constant and painful reminder.

Jimmy has also stopped wondering and asking why and

how he ended up there and who is responsible for him being there.

Sometimes, he hears faint footsteps approaching his cell followed by a soft click, which he has assumed is the safety device that locks the trap-door. Seconds later, this would slide to the left and almost immediately, a wooden tray with a bowl and a latrine would slide in.

Other times, there were no footsteps, further adding to his confusion.

At the beginning, Jimmy would shout and swear, demanding to know where he was, who had abducted him and why. He would bang his fists against the padded walls, the muted sounds of his banging uselessly losing itself in the echoless constraints of the room.

No one ever replied.

Slowly, Jimmy's defiance turned to anguish. The initial threatening tuned into paranoia and the aggressiveness gave way to fear.

Initially, he would walk around the room feeling the walls for some kind of mark, dent or gap, anything that suggested the existence of a door or something to logically explain how he ended up inside that room and as far-fetched as it may have seemed, a way of getting out of there. By any means possible no matter the consequences.

That too proved futile. The fittings were either extremely well padded, negating any chance of finding an opening. Maybe he was dumped from above.

Anything gives Jimmy reason to cry; hunger, body temperature, the need to relieve himself, the lack of memories before his abduction. For that reason, he tries to sleep as much as possible.

He's even given up on trying to escape.

At one point, Jimmy even considered starving himself to death. He started by skipping three meal offers before the hunger pangs became so excruciatingly painful, that he soon resorted to eating his meagre offerings again.

After his ill-attempted hunger strike, Jimmy slowly began to find comfort in the belief of a higher entity, namely, God.

He couldn't remember whether he actually believed or not, however, it now proved comforting. Still aware of all the basic instructions of being a good Christian – doing good deeds, not killing, stealing, or harming anybody, etc. – Jimmy just hadn't the time to practice and fully live by those precepts. Who does nowadays, he thought. Had he, before ending up here? Even that, he couldn't recall. But he knew that wasn't the reason he was there.

All Jimmy knew was, he needed to believe, to have hope, something to look forward to.

Staying alive, at first. Now, death seems a comforting option.

Did he have friends? Probably, the necessary to fulfil his needs. Family? They were there by default.

However, where were they now? Were they missing him or actively looking for him? Did they really care?

Love? As far as he can vaguely recall, it was tormented by nature, demanding at times but love nevertheless.

Who was he in love with? Did he have a girlfriend; was he straight or gay? Not even that he was able to remember. There was this lingering image, of which he was unable to properly make sense. That much he could remember. Is it someone worth returning to if he came out of this alive?

Admittedly, does he still want to stay alive?

As he lay against the padded wall, he heard the faint click from the other side.

Suppertime, I guess.

The small trap-door squeaked as it slid to the left. Soon after, a tray with a faded yellow plastic bowl and a small cup slowly appeared through the gap. Immediately, the trap-door slid to the right shutting out the outside world yet again for Jimmy.

Jimmy got on his knees and pushed himself towards the

tray. He was hungry. To his estimate, the last time he had seen any food must have been twelve hours ago. Working out these estimates still offered some degree of sanity.

Oh shit... again?

Half a loaf of white bread, a thinly cut slice of tomato, a skinny slab of cheese and a cup of water.

This was the third time in a row. Remembering his previous meals also kept him relatively lucid.

However, this time there was no latrine on the tray. It was not the first time this happened.

'Hey! I need to pee!' Jimmy cried out. His voice was broken, frail and very slight, yet it was sufficiently loud to be heard at the other side of his cell.

'Please, can you slide the latrine through? Or a bucket, anything.'

There was no reply.

Why he bothered was anyone's guess. Whenever his mystery captor decided not to include the latrine, Jimmy would go through the same routine. Ask for it. Wait. Then when he couldn't hold it in any longer, he would relieve himself.

This time was no different. He had held in his urine for a few hours but now he could no longer keep it in.

The pain in his bladder had become more and more unbearable. He swore he must have developed, among many other afflictions, some kind of bladder infection.

Once relieved, he held the food bowl in his hand and slowly finished his ration. At least the food, albeit meagre, was still edible.

After placing the bowl and the cup on the tray, Jimmy found a dry patch on the floor. He lay against the wall and did what had lately become his routine.

Cry himself to sleep.

For the first time in a long while, Jimmy woke up feeling colder than usual. Not only cold but also drenched. He opened his eyes. He couldn't see a thing.

He panicked. As much as he squinted, everything was pitch

black. He also realised he was not lying against a soft padded wall. In fact, the surface felt metallic and cold.

Ice cold.

I've been moved.

Jimmy felt too weak to stand. As he rummaged the floor surface with his hands, he also noticed it was hard. And smooth. Concrete, maybe?

How long have I been here?

The last thing he could remember was effortlessly falling asleep after his latest meal. Now, this. Many ideas ran through his head as to how he arrived at this place.

He felt something unfamiliar.

I'm not smelling.

He touched his hair and face with trembling hands. The hair was still long, straw-like, and wet. The beard was still there. He let his hand travel down the rest of his body, feeling his wet skin the lower it went. As he blindly explored his body, not really knowing what to look for, he could feel his scabs, which were now raw and stung at his touch.

He reached his genital area and noticed it was no longer bare. Whoever moved Jimmy had taken the trouble and the decency of fitting some underwear on him. Other than that, he was not wearing anything else.

He huddled against the cold wall. If time seemed endless inside the padded, continuously lit room, it now held a totally unknown dimension in the dark – eerily dark, numbingly silent, and crushingly freezing. Jimmy found it hard to take any comfort from the change in surroundings.

He decided that better than torturing himself awake trying to figure out where he was and why he was now in a dark room, he would try to sleep, in the hope that this was some sort of nightmare or hallucination.

Adopting a foetal position, Jimmy waited until his mind shut off. Something the rest of his body refused to do.

Jimmy was doubly disappointed when he woke up again. One, he was alive. Two, he could still not see a thing.

He straightened up and touched the floor surface for balance. Jimmy leaned against the equally cold wall and got on his knees. He slowly crawled to his left, following the wall's direction until his forehead banged against something hard in front of him. His fingers also hit the same obstacle.

Another wall.

Jimmy calculated he must have crawled some six feet approximately. He turned right. This new wall felt just as cold and damp. He continued to crawl until again, his head banged into another wall. This time he calculated some eight to ten feet. Another right turn.

After crawling what he thought were six feet he stopped. *This must be opposite where I started.* He resumed the crawl and just as he went for the third move, he hit the next wall.

Jimmy turned right again until he finally came to rest where he thought he had begun. The spot on the floor was warmer than the rest of the surface he had crawled.

Whether this exercise in examining his surroundings and proving his lucidity was good or not was academic.

He also realised he had not eaten in almost a day. Jimmy was too tired to feel hungry and soon he drifted into an uneasy but certainly welcome slumber.

'Aaargh!'

Jimmy let out a screeching yell as the hot incandescent rod that woke him from his slumber pierced his eyes. He instinctively shut them again.

He waited a few seconds and tried opening them, this time, squinting carefully.

Again, the white, hot blinding light stung his eyes, piercing through like a molten-hot blade. He turned his head to the left and although his eyes still hurt, the pain was less intense than when he was looking straight at it.

It took some minutes to register what was going on.

He hadn't gone blind, that was evident. Instead, he was back in the padded room. This time, the three minimum wattage bulbs he had grown accustomed to, were replaced by a stadium-like set of floodlights right in front of him. In addition, a loud, purring noise came from the source of the lights.

Once his eyes adjusted to light again, Jimmy tried turning towards the floodlights, but the intensity was too much for him to bear.

'Please, for Christ's sake,' he cried out, 'turn that light off!'

As always, no reply.

'For fuck's sake, why don't you just kill me!' he pleaded, the desperation in his voice thundering above the purring noise of what seemed to be the generator feeding the floodlights.

Jimmy slumped on the padded floor. How could he even attempt to sleep himself to death with this rattle?

Jimmy couldn't remember how much time had passed when he came back to his senses, but now the floodlights were off, the only source of light being the familiar three weak bulbs. No grovelling generator noise, instead, a hellishly deafening silence.

Jimmy found himself in an uncomfortable yet welcome stupor. For the first time since his abduction, he conjured what seemed like coherent images and recollections. Somehow, it felt pleasant.

He left his home in Clarendon Rise, a side street just off Lewisham High Street. It was a late April mid-week morning. He didn't take his car this time. His old 2004 Fiesta that had not only seen better days but probably also better owners, had failed its MOT miserably. Jimmy knew it was a rolling hazard and definitely needed to get rid of it.

The weather had held quite well and a more than pleasant 21° C meant a short sleeve polo shirt, jeans, and suede loafers would definitely not look out of place.

Without notice, as he walked down Albion Way towards the noise, hustle, and bustle of Lewisham market, he felt a sharp prick on his left shoulder.

Drifting in and out of consciousness, he submissively made his way into the back of the van. He walked in, slumped on the floor, and surprisingly allowed his captor to tie up his hands and feet then tape his mouth.

His captor's eyes were dark, mysterious, penetrating, yet at the same time, calm, measured, and soothing, reassuring in as much as they were menacing.

As familiar as those eyes felt, Jimmy was unable to put a face to them. He could picture the features but no familiarity came to mind.

That memory lagoon was slowly drying up but there were still pieces missing. Again, was this a good thing?

Where did it all go so terribly wrong?

It felt cold again. An all too familiar feeling came back to Jimmy. This time, however, he was unable to distinguish his surroundings.

'Jimmy,' he heard a soft whisper, *'are you still here?* A deafening silence followed.

Jimmy opened his eyes but was unable to see anything.

Pitch black. No sound.

It was the same cold, dark vault he had been held in before. He was in a way relieved, he could still recollect places, but at the same time terrified at what he may discover.

'It can be lonely in here, wouldn't you agree Jimmy?'

It took Jimmy a few moments to register the sound.

A voice.

'Who ... who's there?'

There was no sound.

'Where are you? Who's there? What do you want from me?' Jimmy's breath was laboured and his voice pleading.

Still no sound.

It was definitely not a voice inside his head. Or was it?

Maybe this is what dying feels like. If so, no wonder people were so scared of death. Jimmy Kerr on the other hand, had simply grown scared of life. Death could not be any worse than this. You did not need fires and horned creatures with tails, and tridents to experience hell. Hell could be just as dark and cold.

84

And lonely.

'Please,' he said softly, almost crying, 'who are you?'

If he was going to meet his maker, or whoever it was that one meets at the other side, he wanted at least to know why he was checking out in this manner.

'What is it you want from me?'

Not even the breathing of his captor, or whoever had spoken could be heard.

Then suddenly a soft footstep, and immediately after, the clanking noise of what had to be a doorknob broke the deafening silence. Without much warning, a blinding flash of light struck Jimmy, stinging his eyes that had become accustomed to the dark. He let out a shriek.

When his eyes finally adjusted, he saw a bright square at the end of the small room and the silhouette of a stocky man.

He could not distinguish any facial features, just a dark shadow. Tall. Mysterious. Imposing.

With that, the figure climbed out and just as swiftly, shut the door, the loud cavernous clunk devolving darkness back into the cell.

'Wake up.'

An unfamiliar warmth woke Jimmy up. It was the same voice from the dark cell.

This time he was able to see. Blurred, but at least he could see. He was back in the padded room.

'Now slowly get up, we don't want you fainting with the sudden effort.'

Jimmy needed time to adjust, register what was going on, and obey the orders he has just been given.

With his left hand, he covered his eyes while he left the right to cover his private parts. Even in these infrahuman circumstances, the subconscious still has a sense of modesty.

'Jimmy, rejoice,' the gruff voice went on, 'you are finally leaving this room.'

'Who are you?' Jimmy asked.

'Never mind who I am. Just stand up and walk.'

Jimmy was forced to move and walk in front of his captor. There were no instructions, but the body language spoke for itself.

Still naked, he walked through a narrow dimly lit hallway with a door at the end of it.

'Open the door and walk out. Don't even dare look backward.'

Jimmy obeyed silently.

Outside it was mild and a soft breeze blew. A white blanket of clouds covered the sky but didn't look menacing. The whole situation was so confusing and surreal Jimmy Kerr had no time for contemplation. He looked around and took a deep breath. The coughing fit that followed almost made him pass out. Breathing fresh air after such a long time felt unnatural and even painful.

'Go on, walk out. Freedom is something one must never take for granted.'

Jimmy could not agree more.

'Aren't you going to ask me anything?'

Jimmy was acquainting himself with these new surroundings. He did not really know what to do, let alone, what to ask.

'Are you going to kill me?' was all he could think of.

'It has crossed my mind, Jimmy Kerr.'

If now was not the right moment to ask questions, when on earth would be?

'Who are you, why did you kidnap me?'

'I'll first answer the second question. Just don't turn around.'

Jimmy did as told. He simply stood contemplating the scenery. Trees, foliage, sky, clean air.

Freedom.

'I have not kidnapped you...technically speaking,' the gruff-voiced man finally answered. 'When you kidnap someone, you usually ask for a ransom, right?

Jimmy listened, not quite interested in technicalities about a kidnapping.

'Right?' the man repeated.

'Ah, yeah,' Jimmy agreed, not wanting to antagonise his captor, whether it made a difference or not.

'Good. At least we have that concept established.'

'You also asked who I was,' the man continued. 'Wanna take a guess?' A short pause followed, 'still have no idea?'

'No.'

Jimmy's thoughts and ideas were still rather muddled. Not many things of his past had returned.

'Well, I'm not surprised,' the man agreed, 'but that was part of the plan.'

'What,' Jimmy asked, 'to drive me mad?'

'Yes,' the man explained, 'break you down a bit.'

'Break me? But why, what have I done to you?'

The man gave a guttural, deep, tenebrous laugh.

'What do you plan to do with me?'

'I wish I knew myself.'

Suddenly, and not caring what would happen from there on, Jimmy turned round to face his tormentor.

'Well, you do some have balls left Jimmy Kerr.'

Jimmy looked straight into the man's eyes. Dark, mysterious, penetrating, but calm, and measured. They were also sad and melancholic.

'Do you not remember me?'

'I don't.'

'Not surprised. Time can indeed fuck with your head.'

Indeed it could. Had he been told he had been locked up five hundred years, Jimmy would not have argued it.

'Well, I think it is time we made our acquaintances. After being my guest for so long, it is the least I can do.'

'Do you remember Kevin Taylor?'

'Kevin T-Taylor... no mate, don't ring any bell.'

'Hmm,' the man gave a surprised huff. 'This exercise turned out better than I thought.'

Jimmy stared at the man nervously, trying to juggle his memory to no avail.

'Let me tell you a story to refresh your memory.'

The man walked out of the door. 'Please sit against that tree, make yourself comfortable.'

'I am fine standing here.'

'I said, SIT,' his tone menacingly severe.

'I can't. It hurts.'

'If you don't sit down as I tell you, I will break every bone in your body and you will still sit but in worse pain.'

Jimmy acquiesced. The dry leaves and twigs scratched Jimmy's naked and fragile skin, but he was hardly in a position to argue.

'Do you remember Gavin Duncan?'

Jimmy nodded sideways.

'Two years and a month ago, you and that scumbag Gavin did something very awful to young Kevin. You all used to go to the same gym near Mottingham. Kevin had started training as a swimmer while you two fucks just went there to keep fit, which in normal circumstances is not a bad thing.'

Gym, muscles, keeping fit. Jimmy partly recalled something vaguely familiar.

'Still can't remember?'

Jimmy closed his eyes and repeated the name inside his head. *Gavin Duncan. Gavin Duncan.* The name brought back a very distant recollection, but far too removed to help bring back any significant memory.

'You seem at pain trying to remember.'

'I'm afraid it's not coming back.' Jimmy was trembling as he spoke. He was scared not so much by what he didn't know but more about what he feared he would discover.

'I shall continue.'

The man slowly walked towards the tree. Jimmy, in turn, cowered against the tree, encroaching himself defensively.

'No need for that Jimmy boy,' the man said softly. 'I do not intend to hurt you.'

The man sat down opposite Jimmy. 'At least, not now.'

Jimmy looked blankly at him.

'One day, while cutting a stash of cocaine in the dressing

room, someone suddenly came in. You saw Kevin's locker door ajar and in a panic, hid the stash in his rucksack.'

Cocaine, drugs? Jimmy was perplexed but scarily, those two words had a familiar ring to him.

'Yes Jimmy, it seems both you and Gavin were quite naughty. The idea was to retrieve it when the coast was clear, but instead the room just filled up. Only problem was, as bad as you thought you were, you were also rather thick.'

'I don't understand.'

'I'm not surprised!' the man let out a condescending huff.

'Kevin arrived and quite naturally, went into his locker. You had no way of getting your shit back, so you panicked.'

'Who told you all this? How do you know?'

The man did not answer, instead continued the story. 'Unfortunately, Kevin was in a hurry so didn't shower. He simply changed clothes and left for home.'

Jimmy continued to listen, horrified as flashing images returned to him. It seemed he had a not so brilliant and immaculate past.

'You followed the lad with the intention of staging a mugging, nick the rucksack, and run away safely with the stash.'

Jimmy felt as if he'd been dangling from a crane and suddenly someone cut the ropes dropping him free-fall at full speed. The full horror of his true self was fast sinking in, and suddenly he started missing the captivity in the padded cell where the oblivion of time, space, and memory now seemed a safer prospect.

'You ambushed him in the middle of the street, ripped the bag away from him, and looked for the stash. Unfortunately, it was not there. What you two morons hadn't realised was, he had not taken the rucksack where you hid the coke. He had two rucksacks you see, one with his schoolbooks, which is the one he carried and one with his gym stuff that he usually kept in the gym. That is where you hid the drugs.'

Shit.

Jimmy now remembered the moment he and Gavin

savagely mauled the kid. Suffice to say, he now remembered who Gavin was.

'Frustration got the better of you and you punched and kicked Kevin to a pulp. You kicked him so hard, his left eye ended up two inches inside his socket. You broke pretty much every rib and punctured his lungs in three different places. Only because you hadn't realised he was not carrying the rucksack where you hid the drugs. You punished him for your own mistake, your own stupidity.'

Jimmy remembered to his despair, how he cussed and swore at the poor kid. That stash was worth at least 20 grand. His amnesia was no more.

He and Gavin could have returned to the gym, but instead, decided to kick the shit out of that boy.

'For fuck's sake Jimmy, he was only fourteen. He was a still a boy,' Martin choked as he spoke, 'fourteen he was, but still my fucking little baby.'

Jimmy looked up at the man. A single tear trickled down the man's face as he stood, his hands by his side. His look had now turned sad and melancholic.

'My name is Martin. Kevin was my son, Jimmy. He died a slow, painful, and horrendous death. He endured three days of agony.'

Jimmy could now remember as if it had happened yesterday.

'Shit man, we never meant for that to happen,' Jimmy spoke in a nervous staccato, 'we were so pumped up…'

'I feel so much better hearing that,' Martin said sarcastically.

The left side of Jimmy's jaw unexpectedly made its acquaintance with Martin Taylor's right fist. The sound as his facial bone splitting turned his stomach, but he did not react, let alone retaliate.

Jimmy retched in pain but did not utter a sound. Now that he had recovered his memory and with that, rekindled with his violent and less than illustrious past, he was happy to face justice. The justice he had cleverly eluded after killing that boy.

'Hand me in, or kill me, I won't resist, please…'

'No way Jimmy, I won't make it easy for you,' Martin replied, stifling his tears. 'With the way the system works here, they may end up locking me up for abducting you, you may just get away with a caution and even get some compo. Can you imagine?'

'Kill me then.'

'That makes me a murderer.'

Martin knelt down, level with Jimmy Kerr. 'You know, I'm finished. I lost my only son. My marriage went down the shit-hole. It became too much, things were never gonna be the same between my wife and I. You two just fucked up our lives. As it is, I am carrying out one hell of a life sentence.'

Jimmy sat motionless as Martin Taylor produced a gun from his jacket.

'At least this was money well spent.'

Suddenly, Jimmy felt at peace and reconciled. He felt he had more than atoned for his actions during his captivity.

'Just one thing,' Jimmy asked, composed and serene in the knowledge that all would be over. He was, however, curious. 'How did you find out? The Old Bill never caught up with us.'

'Yeah, a bunch of useless fucks they turned out to be,' Martin replied, 'but some digging here and there, helped a bit. You see, everyone has a price. Gavin was an easy catch. What a stupid wanker.' A melancholic yet deranged smile drew on Martin's face. 'Plying him with booze was a piece of cake. He nailed his own coffin, one could say. You, on the other hand, were a bit of hard work, credit to you mate.'

'Just pull the trigger, please.'

'It's not that easy Jimmy. I'm not a murderer.' Martin cocked back the safety release. His hands were trembling.

'Just do it.'

Jimmy opened his arms and shut his eyes.

'It's just not fair,' Martin's voice grew bitter. 'Whatever I do, I'm screwed. You took away my son, ruined my marriage and now you're gonna get away scot-free, you little son of a bitch.'

'Just do it, Kevin.'

'It's Martin you fucking twat!' Martin yelled.

Martin's hands were sweaty. He sat next to Jimmy holding the gun with both hands and placed the weapon against his temple. Satisfied the gun was in the right place and no chance of missing, Martin slowly pulled back the trigger.

The shot went out with a muffled bang. The cracking noise of the skull exploding as the bullet exited the head was sickening as was the splattering of brain matter hitting against the tree.

The real sentence had only just begun.

MALAGA VIRGEN

There's a wise old tale, from the same old hell
Only the devil is changed
Different devil - Chickenfoot

They say a picture is worth a thousand words. What lies imprisoned within that photo, postcard, canvas, or as it is nowadays, a Smartphone screen, is up to the beholder's eye to decipher.

El Pimpi, a true Malaga institution, was quite full for a Tuesday night.

This was supposed to be my last night in this, if not romantic, nevertheless charming city. As I drank my way through the different local wines at one of the bar areas that snake around this place, two almost empty wine flutes caught my attention.

Almost empty, but by no means finished.

The dark amber-like concoction still contained in those flutes was hard to make out – maybe sherry, possibly Amontillado, or Fino.

The positioning of these glasses, however, caught my eye. There was a special vibe about them – or probably an excess of sweet wine running through my system. Side by side they stood, waiting, unfinished, yet certainly not ownerless.

Yes, ownerless they certainly were not. The couple who had been imbibing from these flutes had just stepped away, probably admiring the memorabilia pasted on the wall opposite, depicting previous celebrity visitors to this iconic place.

From the edge of the bar, a couple of feet away, I had a good view of them without being intrusive, as they returned to the bar.

They sat, resting their elbows on the bar and slowly grabbed each other's hand. He said something to her; she listened attentively, eyes glued to his every word. Her look was tender, sweet, and youthful. His gaze, while definitely masculine, was equally sweet and tender as they drew closer and kissed.

He was probably around five foot seven, regular build; very short brown hair peppered with a generous amount of grey, square jaw and a day's stubble maybe. Despite his rigid and sharp features, his expression was relaxed and very much at ease. To be honest, with such a beautiful companion, who could hold a hard, stern face for long? Light brown jeans, a light blue long-sleeve linen shirt, and white trainers completed his attire.

She was attractive in a mature and classy way, considerably shorter yet very well proportioned. Her hair was light brown, long and wavy. Blue jeans neatly matched with a slightly loose short sleeve grey GAP T-shirt, enough to tease the imagination into guessing what lay underneath. She had piercing green eyes and like her companion, she wore a relaxed and soft expression on her face. Unlike him though, her lines were soft and perfectly rounded.

They conjured something hidden, mysterious, forbidden, yet genuine and pure. Their glasses refused to be finished, clinging on to the last drop as if it were a lifeline.

Still holding hands, their conversation briefly interrupted by a spontaneous kiss, he softly caressed her fingers while she, looking up at him, devolved his caresses with equal tenderness.

A few moments later, they got up and started taking pictures of each other against the backdrop of celebrity photos, some famous, others less so, that had visited this bar in the past.

Ah, the magic of instant photography.

Very casually, I drew out my Smartphone, immediately capturing those two half-empty but not yet finished flutes of wine. Imprisoned within the pixel-filled confines of my Smartphone, I probably had the greatest love story yet to be told.

It was the most perfect picture I had captured in one take!

No doubt, they looked very much in love, content and extremely in touch with each other's feelings. However, a shroud of secrecy and melancholy hung over them.

After exchanging some words here and there, silence took over and I caught them again gazing into each other's eyes, still holding hands.

Where true love exists, a silent stare speaks volumes; a simple touch is worth more than a thousand beautifully manicured words.

I travel an awful lot because of my job. I have been fortunate enough to visit many exciting places, full of culture, history, stories to tell. It is, however, in the most inconspicuous of cities, those one would call boring, that I usually find the most interesting tales.

Yes, exciting and popular places certainly have their charm; they don't call them tourist traps for nothing. But, go off the beaten track, somewhere without the monument, the history, the charm, and you end up digging up its hidden charm, rewriting your own history, sometimes even erecting some unique monument.

Malaga, for all its allure for the Northern European tourist, its benign climate, friendly people and being a gateway to the hip coastal resorts of the *Costa del Sol,* has its share of attractions. Nevertheless, as charming as it is, it doesn't immediately associate with romance. Then again, love cares little for geographic boundaries.

They say expectations are the bane of happiness. Then again, this sometimes ungrateful job of mine hardly helps making friends along the way and happiness usually eludes me like the plague.

Last night, however, friendless as I was, I found happiness. Two strangers in love – whether for the right or wrong reasons but very much in love.

How's that for expectations?

Very discretely, feigning to read a message on my phone – oh, modern technology saving the moment! – I snapped away and froze another moment for posterity.

And my client.

After checking my digital masterpiece, I noticed he was gone. She was studying the photos on the wall, yet keeping a guarded eye on their still unfinished drinks.

She was stunning I still have to admit. I almost envied that man.

A minute or so later, he returned, visibly relieved. Taking her hand, they returned to their stools and two wine glasses.

Simultaneously, both he and I raise our hands to summon the waiter. In an act of gallantry and good manners, I gesture for the couple to be served first.

They both nodded in gratitude and smiled. His was appreciative and almost carried a sense of camaraderie. Hers was sweet, gentle, innocent.

It was a good idea I let them order first. As I waited to be served, I heard the man order two more of the same drinks.

I noticed then he was not Spanish. Neither was his partner.

But that, I already knew.

'Dos *Málaga Virgen*, por favor,' he told the waiter.

So that's what it was! Mystery solved.

'Deme lo mismo,' I discretely told the barman when my turn arrived.

That drink definitely had something about it. It's sweet, velvety, syrupy texture certainly invites mischief, passion, and God knows what else, given the right amount.

Definitely a drink for lovers.

Ok, maybe that was an ambitious assumption but, what did I say about creating your own magic moment in lesser-known destinations?

I timed my drinking to that of this mysterious couple. I was right all along; as much at ease, as they seemed, there was something untoward about them.

My job here was almost done. I had an early flight next morning, so I needed to wrap things up.

Outside *El Pimpi*, I blended with the crowd ambling through Calle Alcazabilla, bidding my time.

Finally, half an hour after I left, my charges walked out the main door, hand in hand, still as blissfully in love as I had left them. A perfect photo opportunity.

One more for the record.

Hat-trick!

ANT RICHARDS

I followed them from a safe distance, shielded by my cream overcoat and my Fedora, resembling a 21st Century Bogart-esque character.

They stopped to admire the beautifully lit Roman Amphitheatre at the foot of the no less impressive Alcazaba. Even I found it hard not to find this iconic edifice impressive.

Lovingly clutching each other's hand, they continued walking towards Alameda Principal, the main thoroughfare of downtown Malaga.

They reached a bus stop, and very hurriedly, embarked on a kiss. I watched from the other side of the avenue

Cars were passing from both directions, however, whenever there was a gap, I still saw them both locked in the same kiss. I'm sure it was the same one – no one separates from those kinds of kisses.

A few minutes after, a number '3' bus pulled in.

Bollocks!

What the hell was I doing on this side of the avenue?

Too late. Alameda Principal was too busy to attempt crossing.

Standing helpless, I felt the complete idiot. I couldn't hail a cab, and tell the driver, 'Hey, follow that bus!' and hope to catch up. That only happens in films.

The bus pulled out and I stood horrified watching it slowly take to the avenue.

As I cursed my stupid timing, I lifted my gaze and there he stood, a more deject look on his face than I wore a few seconds back.

He slowly walked towards the closest traffic light to his left. Relieved, I watched him cross towards my side and head to the first bus stop.

I cautiously walked towards the bus stop.

Not long after, the 173 bus pulled up and he, together with two elderly ladies boarded. I waited until there was no one left to board before jumping on myself.

He alighted after the fifth stop. Cautiously, and at a safe distance, I followed him to his hotel, opposite María Zambrano Train Station.

I only had this one chance.

Fortunately, this fool seemed too damn upset to notice he was being followed. It's amazing how a lovely face, a few kisses, and the appropriate words can cloud a man's senses.

Bypassing the reception desk, he headed straight for the lifts.

'Excuse me, Sir,' I caught him just before the doors opened, 'can I trouble you just a couple of minutes?' A blunt approach yet still courteous.

He turned nervously, surprised.

In my line of work, an element of surprise is crucial.

'Yes, how can I help you?' There was a hint of hesitation despite his assertiveness, 'and how do you know I speak English?'

'I know many things about you, Sebastian,' I wasted no time in useless pleasantries, 'and you'd be surprised how much I know about Isabella.'

He froze and swallowed hard.

'We need to talk. Now.'

'Why would we need to talk?'

'Because I fucking say so.'

A bucket of ice-cold water could not have had a better effect. Nice to see my standards hadn't slipped.

'And who the fuck are you when you're at home?' He obviously still had some fight left.

'I can be many things to you. But get cocky and I can be a proper bastard.'

He didn't reply.

I left the uncomfortable silence to linger between us. It was definitely speaking volumes.

I walked past the reception desks towards the bar area on the other side of the foyer. With no need to usher him over, Sebastian followed a few steps behind.

I took a seat by the long, tall window, just past the bar area. With a slight nod, I indicated he took the seat in front of me.

'Ok... you wanted to talk?' Sebastian finally broke the silence.

I studied his face. He showed neither fear nor aggression.

I offered a wry smile as I looked to my left, making sure that the people closest to us were not within hearing distance.

'Ok then, can we cut the crap? You clearly know who I am, and it seems you've got quite a bit on Isabella.'

Feeding into other's fear, anxiety, and curiosity does help get people where I want them.

'Sebastian, son,' I stretched the sentence for effect, 'messing about with a married woman can be dangerous shit...'

Sebastian fidgeted his fingers nervously.

'My client is not very happy, you know. What you are doing is not nice. People get hurt in the end.'

I let an uncomfortable silence set the mood.

'By the way, is that *Malaga Virgen* really any good?'

'Try it for yourself.'

'I am trying to be friendly.'

'Go fuck yourself.'

I do hate it when people tell me to go fuck myself. 'If I were you, I'd be nicer to me, you know. I've kneecapped people for much less than this.'

'What the fuck are you? Marcel De Cassis sent you or something?'

'I do not answer to you, but I can decide whether you walk properly after tonight or not so don't fuck with me, Sebastian.'

Without giving him a chance to react, I quickly grabbed his hand and squeezed it until the brittle sound of his bones made *me* shiver.

He grimaced in pain but said nothing. I continued to hold his hand until mine was hurting.

'Now, we are going to talk. Nicely. Is that clear?'

Sebastian offered me the most hideous and hateful look but nodded in agreement. I slowly release his hand.

'Good. I like it when we have an understanding.'

Under different circumstances, I could have achieved quicker results using some proper South East London hospitality, but that was not part of the deal. I was not supposed to hurt him – at least, not physically.

'What is it you want then?'

'I thought you'd never ask.'

'So...?'

'Tell me, why Isabella?'

Sebastian took a deep breath. 'You probably know better than me, being the clever dick you appear to be.' He was still up for some confrontation.

How brave. And stupid.

'I'm warning you. Don't push it...'

He told me about how they met years ago, how foolishly he let her go. He went on about mistakes, regrets, and all that jazz. The usual soppy, boring, love bollocks.

I could understand why he was so crazy about Isabella de Cassis. She is definitely a decent fuck, but shit, they're both married, living in different countries...why fucking complicate things?

'A bit late for regrets, wouldn't you think?'

Love is so fucking blind.

'So why do you think she doesn't leave Mr. De Cassis?'

'Ask your fucking client.'

I sometimes get so tired of this 'I'm so brave' shit. 'Didn't I tell you to be nice to me?'

Sebastian sighed and rubbed his forehead with his index finger. He was getting agitated.

And I impatient.

'And what do you intend to do? Continue these illicit meetings, live the lie, love in hiding? Gimme a break!'

Sebastian sat silently, digesting my response.

A civil servant back home in Lewisham Council, how could he possibly compete with Mr. De Cassis, a rich wine magnate with money pouring out his pores as well as his arse. What could Isabella, beautiful and stunning as she was, see in him?

'I can't answer that.'

I didn't think he could.

'Look here,' time to add insult to injury. 'I've been paid stupid money to follow you two, I reckon... about four times your monthly wages? Hang on a sec.'

Taking my Smartphone from my blazer's pocket, I flicked through my photo gallery, showing pictures of him, his kids, and his wife. 'Nice family you got,' I continued until reaching the ones I'd been taking since they arrived in Malaga, including those at *El Pimpi*. 'You got one colourful file here mate. I can screw you big fucking time.'

Sebastian's breathing accelerated as I scrolled through the damaging evidence. I reckoned the point was clear by then.

'I show this shit here, and you're fucked forever.'

'You bastard!' He scoffed.

'I've been called much worse, you've no idea.'

I smiled at him.

'Believe me, I enjoy this job.'

'Look here, I don't want Isabella harmed because of this.'

'As if I gave a shit,' I scratched the stubble on my chin. It felt soothing. 'I've been paid to do a job, and I've all the intention of seeing it through.'

I could feel his life, as he knew it, beginning to crumble around him. Whatever he did now, he was screwed. I was already picturing my next holiday when I got paid.

'Can't we reach some kind of arrangement,' Sebastian was desperate, 'you and me?'

'I doubt it Sebastian – and that's the beauty of it.' I could feel he wanted to smash my face in. Who could blame him? However, I was enjoying the moment. I know, shameless, but that's what I'm like...

'Sebastian, you couldn't ever afford to make a counteroffer. However...'

I saw a glint of hope in his eyes, his body language ripe for negotiating. You can only yield a good deal when the other party is down and vulnerable.

Besides getting paid handsomely, I thought I'd see what I

could rub off this arsehole as well.

'You really love this bird?'

'What?' Sebastian looked puzzled.

'Isn't my fucking English good enough? I asked you a question.'

'Yes, I do love her.'

'Then maybe we can reach some arrangement. Three weeks Sebastian.'

'Three weeks?'

'Is there a fucking echo in this room?'

'You have three weeks to tell your wife you're leaving her; three weeks to convince Isabella to become the future ex-Mrs De Cassis. Essentially, three weeks to get your arse in gear and sort your shit out, once and for all.'

'What?'

'Oh fuck! Are you deaf as well as thick?'

I was knackered. At that point, I could have murdered a drink – but certainly not a Málaga Virgen.

'You're taking the piss...'

'You see me laughing or smiling?'

'That's fucking crazy...' I thought he'd start hyperventilating.

'C'mon, where there's a will... three weeks.'

'How do I know you're not bullshitting me?'

'You don't, you see,' this was the fun part. 'My job is done. I'll still get paid regardless. You, well...you're fucked. Sorry.' I wasn't really, but well, I do have traces of decency in me, '... that was part of the deal. But here's the thing, I'm giving you a lifeline.'

Sebastian seemed finally eager to weigh his options.

'It's a gamble I know, but I'd say it's worth it, given your position. Own up, and shit might even brighten up. Just imagine, finally, you and Isabella can shag legally ever after!'

I stood and walked toward Sebastian – at this point, I could tell he was broken. But I'd given him a way out.

I know, terribly nice of me.

'Three weeks... and I have you both on the watch. If it's not me, believe me, there'll be a... guardian angel watching over you.'

Without exchanging any further pleasantries, I walked out of the hotel.

Shit, playing the Devil's advocate is hard work sometimes.

This particular job, I admit, was a strange one. But what is life without challenges? At my age, I can ill afford complacency. Inefficiency can eventually render me unemployed, penniless.

Did I grow a conscience in the end?

Far from that.

In the end, money is what drives me. I completed my job.

Consequences? Nothing to do with me. Yes, I may have added a little twist – then again, one is entitled to a little fun, right?

Isabella De Cassis, you are twisted, devious, scheming, but a fucking genius. What a formidable client you turned out to be.

THE DEVIL YOU KNOW

I'm not just the one you think you see (Today I'm gonna look one way, the one they should know)
Can't you see the other side of me?(Tonight you're gonna see me change, and not just my clothes)

Shape - Saga

Sam finally managed to relax. Never one to justify his actions, lately, however, he's been making up too many excuses for his late homecomings. Tonight should have been different. However, temptation triumphed over prudence, so he needed to think a way of keeping strife and tribulations to a minimum on the home front.

The home front's name is Vanessa Harding. At 37, she is still exceptionally attractive, even if a good proportion of that beauty is surgically enhanced. With slightly oversized breasts and a near perfect pearly facial complexion, she is the perfect prize for Sam Harding despite the massive disproportion between what surgery had managed to improve against what she has for brains. Sam, however, is quite happy with that minor shortcoming. The last thing a man like him needs is a clever wife.

Louise, on the other hand, is a different story – uncomplicated yet demanding, ridiculously high maintenance and diabolically hot.

A diverse portfolio of pawn shops, barbers, ethnic cafés, second-league casinos, shark-loan establishments, and a number of old housing used for low-rent accommodation make up the bulk of his business empire covering the Lewisham, Brockley and New Forest areas.

To keep profits generous and hassle-free, the promise of broken bones and cramped horizontal dwellings usually help keep inconveniences to a minimum. But despite being one of the undisputed kingpins of Southeast London's underworld, Sam does make sure not to be legally associated with some of these shoddy practices.

'Come on sugar bun, why don't you have a drink and just chill?' Louise said lying invitingly on the oversized queen bed, toying with her champagne flute, wearing nothing more than very arousing black-laced lingerie.

Sam and Louise's rendezvous usually involve fine champagne, fine dining, and a fine suite at a no less than a fine five-star hotel.

'Shit Lu, what I need is a fucking stiff whisky,' Sam snapped back as he scratched his neck in front of the mirror. He had had a lousy day. The long arm had visited one of his fast-loan premises following a complaint from one of his customers. Then, a hand-basin in one of the flats he lets had caved in and surprisingly enough, the tenant was demanding to have it fixed immediately. Some people, it seems, want good value for money all the time.

Fortunately, Keith Langley, his legal advisor – and occasional fixer – was available to dispel any potential bother.

Sam was looking forward to a quiet end of the day. Until of course, Louise called.

'Whisky! Urgh!' Louise cried back, 'you can have your whisky when you're out with the boys, talking business or plotting your plans of Southeast London domination!'

Sam turned and stared at Louise, giving her a crooked smile.

'Come over big boy and have another glass of champers with me. For once, try to be sophisticated.'

'Sophisticated, pah!' he spat back, still smiling. 'Bubbly is for birds and barbies. Even Keith who can be a bit of a softie now and then,' he smirked, 'wouldn't be seen holding a glass of that shit.'

Sam held Keith in very high esteem. They've worked together for almost twenty years. While Sam had a persuasive personality (remember broken bones and all that), Keith had the legal expertise to know how far they could flex their muscle. And other people's bones.

'You speak so sweetly of him, yet you have no problem banging his wife.'

'That's because she's a tart.'

Sam was well aware it was technically wrong to be shagging his partner's wife, but then, Louise was too feisty a creature; ignoring her advances were hardly an option. Anyway, what the eyes don't see...

'Yeah... and remind me who comes running at the snap of a finger?'

'A fit and clever tart though. That, I admit.'

Sam got rid of his boxer shorts, clambered over the bed and buried himself under the covers, as Louise welcomed him with open arms. And open legs.

After watching the first twenty minutes of *I'm a celebrity...get me out of here!* Vanessa became bored and restless. She didn't mind Sam running business meetings – or whatever he called them – into the small hours, but lately, these meetings were becoming too frequent for her liking. However, as long as her credit cards' limits were beyond sensible reach, who was she to question him?

They had two boys, Lester and Mansfield who were almost in their twenties. Soon they would be taking care of themselves it seemed, following their dad's footsteps as well. Not what she had planned for them, but they could do much worse.

Vanessa switched off the TV and headed to the conservatory. As she gazed out to the garden where she couldn't see much at this time of night, she convinced herself she could do with a drink. Or three. She could also do with some company.

Any company.

Sam was lying lazily on his back against two large pillows; his heavy arms slumped to his sides, his steely blue eyes staring at the ceiling and a slight frown on his face.

'So darling, what's troubling you up there?' Louise took yet another sip of champagne as she tapped on Sam's temple, 'you seem a bit edgy tonight, anything wrong?'

Sam turned, he pinched her left nipple and bit her earlobe.

'Nah, just had a shitty day, that's all,' he cupped his hands behind his head. 'That wanker earlier on, so desperate to borrow that grand, and now giving us shit to keep up with his repayments...'

'Well at what, 500% interest, I'm not surprised.'

'Then they shouldn't get into so much fucking debt now, innit?'

'What happened in the end?'

'Aw, the usual, lovely Keith did his little sweet talk thingy.'

'He knows how to say the right thing at the right time, innit?' Louise feigned incredulity.

'Louise,' Sam dragged the '...ise' longer than necessary, 'you know we shouldn't mix business with pleasure, now.'

Louise just rolled her eyes, gave a soft complicit laugh, buried herself against Sam's right side and started massaging below his navel. He returned the gesture grabbing and squeezing her buttocks.

'Wouldn't it be funny if Keith and Vanessa were doing the same thing as us?' Louise said playfully.

'If I find out I'd rip Keith's balls out with me bare hands and feed them to Vanessa,' Sam replied, while he buried his head between her breasts.

'You clearly don't believe in equality, do you?'

'Of course, I do. Just not for other people,' he got up from the bed. 'Anyway, going for a piss,' he accompanied the announcement with a slight but emphatic fart.

'Oh Sam, your sweetness is legendary...'

Heath's Lounge was unusually busy for a midweek night in Blackheath. Vanessa arrived by minicab. Although she held her drink quite well and wasn't planning on going on a bender, she could ill afford any unwanted questioning should something unexpected happen while behind the wheel.

Callum Doherty was already at the bar, an oversized, tacky, and girly looking cocktail glass rocking in his right hand as he chatted with an equally tacky and oversized girl.

What a prat. Vanessa waved at him as she approached the bar.

'Van!'

'Cal.'

He got off the stool and greeted her with a kiss, slightly closer than necessary to her lips. 'Can we be a bit more discreet?' Vanessa whispered as she offered a perfunctory smile to the oversized girl, which was the equivalent of telling her to piss off.

They both retired to a corner of the bar. 'Can you get me a glass of Prosecco, Marius?'

Marius, the South African barman on duty, acknowledged with a gentle nod.

'Actually,' Callum caught him as he was about to turn, 'can we have a bottle?'

Marius hardly complained at this upgraded request as he walked to the freezer.

'You haven't called me in weeks, you been ok?'

'Been busy darling. Anyway, tell you what.' Vanessa loosened her pastel blue pashmina, releasing a whiff of Dior's Poison. 'Do you mind if we go somewhere quieter after we down this bottle?'

'Of course,' Callum *discreetly* grabbed her hand under the bar table, 'anything for my princess.'

Amazing what the promise of free pussy can do, she sighed.

Sam slumped on the bed when he returned from the loo. Relieved, satisfied, but exhausted and worn out, he noticed he was finding it hard keeping up with Louise.

And Keith, poor ol' bastard, has to put up with this on a regular basis!

Louise was playing around with the remote control until she found a station that finally played a song she fancied: Lady Gaga's *Poker Face*.

Sam lay quietly smoking a cigarillo, making circles with the smoke every time he exhaled.

'What time do you have to go home to Vanessa, luv,' Louise asked as she caressed his forehead.

'No rush Lu... whenever appropriate. What time is your movie over?'

'In about another hour, I guess,' she replied yawningly.

'Guess you're cabbing it home then, right?'

'Keith can't see me arriving in your car now, can he?'

'That would be... inappropriate, wouldn't it?'

Louise buried herself under the sheets and Sam let out a

contained grunt as her hair tickled his nether regions. Life was fucking good and Sam was happy.

Happy, but worn out.

Callum was lying against the wall behind what was usually Sam's desk, a contemptuous smirk drawn on his lips. *If only you could see me, you smug little bastard*, he smiled at a picture of Sam riding his black Harley Davidson.

Six years back, Sam Harding, in a shrewd stroke of business acumen, made a hostile takeover of Callum Doherty's then successful minicab firm *Cal's Cars*. Shrewd in the sense that no money exchanged hands; hostile as in arms becoming fractured, noses swollen, eyes blackened and threats issued when negotiations stalled.

Vanessa Harding, well documented on the incident, always thought her husband's brute business methods verged on the sickening – even if they helped finance her lavish lifestyle – and took pity on Callum when they unexpectedly met over a year ago. The fact that he is also an asshole of immeasurable proportions hardly made a difference when she started flirting with him.

After pulling up her knickers then pulling down her dress, Vanessa checked her phone. 'I think it's time we made a move sweetie,' she grabbed her handbag and slid on her gloves, then knelt down beside Callum and started kissing him.

'Sorry we had to make this a quickie Cal.' Vanessa kissed around his neck, while her hands explored below his waistline.

'That's alright,' he replied between grunts as her hand rubbed against his nuts and manhood through his underpants. 'Although I'd prefer if you'd let go of your phone while I fucked you, it's a bit, like... off-putting, y'know what I mean?'

'Oh come on, since when are you so romantic?'

Callum didn't answer, but slid his hand through her bra and squeezed her breast, pulling her towards him with his left hand.

'Anyway, knowing Sam, if he messages me and I don't reply fast, he gets all panicky and, well, best not to get on his wrong foot.'

Vanessa knelt between his outstretched legs, got better purchase on his bulge, while Callum's two hands slid under her knickers and squeezed her ass, bringing her closer to him, her handbag now dangling from her neck the only thing separating their chests. 'Anyway, Van, hope you find these photos useful.'

'Absolutely, sweetie pie.' Her left hand moved her bag out of the way while the other hand now worked faster on him as they kissed each other's breath away.

At the end of Vanessa's masterstroke, Callum gave out a contained groan, let his hands go, and collapsed. A truly breathtaking experience.

Sam thanked the valet as he exchanged a ten-pound note for his car keys. He opened the door for Louise and went to the right side to take his place at the wheel.

They left the palatial Manor Green hotel in Greenwich and headed towards Maze Hill. At the end, Sam turned right into Prince Charles Road, finally leading to Montpelier Row.

There was a bit of traffic as they approached the centre of Blackheath Village. He stopped just behind the bus stop opposite Blackheath Train station where Louise alighted. They kissed goodbye and as soon as she could, she crossed the road and walked down the car park adjacent to the station where there is a minicab office.

Sam was about to pull out when his Smartphone started buzzing hysterically. It wasn't a phone call, but a series of incoming messages.

Keith parked his black 2010 Audi A4 and checked his phone again for any messages before leaving his car.

There was nothing.

A faint light from one of the back rooms at their office glimmered.

The street was deserted, save for the occasional car swishing through the almost quiet High Street. He clicked on his car fob to lock the doors and slowly crossed the street. It was still a relatively mild evening.

Upstairs at the office, Vanessa greeted Keith at the door.

'Awright me lovely,' he said in his East London drawl, 'can you tell me what yer panic's all about?'

'Actually,' Vanessa ushered Keith in and shut the door behind him, 'better see for yourself.'

Keith's jaw dropped at the sight of Callum Doherty slumped against the wall behind Sam's desk, the paper cutter still embedded in his abdomen, with a line of blood running down his shirt. With the fly of his trousers still unzipped, the sight of his now useless manhood protruding from his underpants rammed a series of unthinkable questions through Keith's mind.

'What the fuck happened here Van?'

'He got a bit fresh with me. Well, more than he should have anyway.'

Keith pointed at Callum's still evident erection, 'it seems he probably had a good sending off before you shut him down.'

She explained to Keith how she discovered Sam was having an affair with his wife. To support her claims, she produced some revealing pictures taken by Callum himself.

'It's been going on for some time, you know,' Vanessa sat on the edge of Sam's desk, bitter tears flooding her green eyes. 'I know you men struggle to keep your dicks in your pants at best, so it's disappointing in a way, but, that I can cope with,' she continued unable to hold back her sobbing. 'But when you find out your man's sleeping with your fucking best friend...'

'Are you absolutely sure? How do I know you're not bullshitting me?'

'Was she at home when you came here?'

Keith gripped his hands, his face reddened, 'Ok, we're no fucking saints, but Sam and Lou... '

'I'm sorry to say this Keith, as much as I liked Louise, she's always had a tendency for being a bit loose down here. As for Sam ...'

'After all I've fucking done for him...'

'Including softening Callum up back in the day...'

'Ah, you er, know about that?'

113

'I may have my blonde streaks but I'm not that stupid,' she got up and straightened her dress and ran her fingers through her streaks of hair still stuck to her forehead.

'So... you and Callum, what was that all about?'

Vanessa blew her nose, gave a couple of sniffs, and straightened herself on the desk. 'In a way, I was getting back at Sam, but mainly, gathering evidence. Cal was good at surveillance and stuff.'

'Oh he was, now... that slipped from our radar,' Keith frowned, mentally cursing himself for not keeping an eye on him after their successful business venture. 'So Van, the body...'

'You are the fixer Keith. C'mon, I can't stand the way Cal's staring at us.'

'Hmm, I'd now like to see our Sam stare at us just like that.'

Vanessa gave a weak smile but didn't reply.

'Do you think they're together right now?'

'Do I think?' Vanessa Harding flapped her hands in the air, barely brushing Keith's face, 'They're probably on their second or third shag right now. Although knowing Sam's performance lately, I'd say struggling on the second.'

Keith bit his upper lip until he almost drew blood, struggling to keep his hands from crumpling the photos.

Vanessa lit a cigarette, offering one to Keith.

'Not in here love. 'ealth n' safety an' all that.'

Vanessa gave him a disdained look and shook her head.

'So Keith,' Vanessa blew out a fine plume of smoke to Keith's added annoyance, 'the body?'

He shrugged his shoulders, 'Dunno... first you call me in, then the body, Sam and Lou... all this is too fucking much. I can't even fucking think straight now.'

'Come. I think I can help you de-stress a little.'

Sam scrolled through the pictures again and again. And again.

How could Callum Doherty be so stupid? Trying to blackmail me, after all he'd lost and gone through a few years back.

114

He must have a fucking death wish or something, he thought. Sam's first impulse would be to call Keith, but given the circumstances...

In fact, Keith could well become a liability right now.

Worst-case scenario, Keith was expendable. It would break Sam's heart, but he'd live. Keith, maybe not.

Louise? Well, he could sweet talk his way out of trouble with her.

Vanessa? He'd probably have to increase her allowance.

Keith knew he'd crossed a sacred line. In this industry, it's a definite no-no.

Then again, fucking his soon-to-be ex-boss's wife was something he couldn't *not* enjoy. Old school as he was, Keith had always regarded Vanessa with the utmost respect. There was no doubt Vanessa was fit, pretty – albeit, with the odd surgical enhancement here and there – and quite sexy, but she was a taken woman at the end of the day.

Pinned against her husband's desk, Keith fucked Vanessa with a raw, savage, vengeful lust he never thought he could work up. At the same time, he was also devising a way to pin Callum's murder on Sam.

Vanessa, on the other hand, enjoyed the idea of cheating on one of Lewisham's toughest, most ruthless underground *Supremo's* with his lackey and a former business rivals. She was shameless about giving herself to Keith, despite never regarding him that highly, but when needs must...

'Shit Keith! You didn't need much convincing,' Vanessa straightened up, rubbed her belly, looking at the marks left by the pen, a calculator and other loose object lying on the desk as Keith pinned her down. She straightened her dress and turning towards Keith, she whispered, 'we definitely know each other well now...'

Keith gave a wry smile back, and was about to apologise but instead said, 'Nothing personal sweetheart.'

'I know,' Vanessa smacked a kiss on his lips.

Vanessa went to their bathroom to wash her face and tidy

her hair, making sure her clothes were not too crumpled. 'I know you guys are not big on the entertainment side with clients, but surely you could afford a more decent toilet,' she remarked with some disgust. 'Anyway, I got to go now in case Sam's on his way home,'

'You gonna be ok?'

'Trust me, I'm well covered.'

Keith was not sure in what context she meant that.

Just as Sam was ready to turn the ignition, he realised that not only had he received all these pictures on his phone by WhatsApp, they also came in on his business email address, so surely these would also appear on his laptop.

At the office.

Keith took all of a couple of minutes to tidy up the evidence of his rendezvous with Vanessa.

He took another look at the incriminating photos of Sam and Louise, which included snaps of them in Sam's car, entering hotel receptions, leaving them, as well as others a tad more graphic. Those that don't necessarily include clothes.

Keith's rage slowly turned to cold and sinister plotting. At least, Keith had already exacted his just revenge. One he'd be happy to repeat given half a chance.

It was past ten o'clock. Louise would be back from her 'movie' but Keith was in no hurry to go back home. He was happy to spend all night in the office and greet Sam next morning. Would he take Sam for a walk? Nah, he thought, too cliché and also very risky, knowing his boss.

The scene had to be perfect if he were to frame Callum's murder on Sam. After, he'd need to make sure that when he's checked into Pentonville or Woodworm Scrubs Hilton, their Guest Relations would make Sam's stay a memorable one.

He walked over to the cabinet, poured himself a generous fix of Sam's finest malt then went back to his desk and made himself comfortable.

He switched off the light and snuggled comfortably at his

desk. The night was still young.

'Here,' he raised his glass, 'to future absent friends.'

Sam had to juggle the key before the cylinder finally turned, opening the door to his office.

It was five minutes to eleven.

Instinctively, Sam switched on the light, only to be greeted by his henchman.

Startled as he was to see Keith in the office, he wasn't at all surprised. Just scared.

Chicken-shit-scared.

Did Keith already know? If so how much, and how did he find out? How the fuck was he going to react?

Should he put Keith out of his misery – thus, relieving himself of some unnecessary bother as well? What if this was all a trap? Was Keith already armed?

Sam Harding was fucking scared!

'Keith mate, what's up? 'you doing here at this time of night?'

'We got us an intruder in the office,' he nodded at Callum Doherty, lying undignified behind the boss's desk, his dick still peeping out of his unzipped trousers.

Yeah, right. An intruder.

'memeber'im? Ol' Callum Doherty? Seems he woz snoopin' around.' Keith was still sat, stretched out at his desk.

'Er yes, I remember that Irish cunt,' Sam tried to sound as gruff as always, 'anyway... how d'ya know he was here?'

'I didn't... I woz driving past on me way home from Tesco's and while I was waiting at the traffic lights, I just looked up, as you do, and I noticed the lights were on in the office. I got suspicious, stopped the car, looked to see if I saw yours... you know, sorting out shit into the hours as you sometimes do. I called, but your phone went straight to voicemail...'

Of course, I was banging your wife...

'... so I just parked and came upstairs. Caught the 'ol fucker 'aving a go at yer computer and...'

'Ok, but what was he doing here, I mean, before you beat

the shit out of him – which I presume you did – did he tell ya?'

'That's the thing, Sam,' Keith paused for a few seconds, 'didn't have time... he got all shirty and shit and, well, I think I may 'ave gone a bit too 'ard on 'im.'

'Oh fuck...' Sam wasn't sure whether to be relieved or even more scared. 'So you just, like... killed him.'

Keith simply shrugged. 'Din't mean to, y' know, shit happened, dunno... maybe I overreacted, that's all.'

Overreact? Since when do you overreact, Keith? He would calmly snip off the tip of Callum's fingers before killing him. And he would do it slowly and meticulously. That was the professionalism Sam so liked about Keith. And now, scared the shit out of him.

It was clear both suspected each other now. But neither was sure nor confident in making the first move.

This promised to be one long mother of a night.

Sam scanned the office, keeping a watchful eye on Keith. He crouched next to Callum's body. For some inexplicable reason, he put his index and middle finger on the near rigid, cold neck. Not that he needed confirmation the kid was stiff, but maybe more out of incredulousness. He noticed the cause of death still sticking out of his abdomen.

Thinking he recognised the origin of the killer weapon, he bent the handle to check.

'That's my paper cutter.' He turned and cranked his neck at Keith, still sitting opposite his desk.

'A paper cutter? You killed him with a paper cutter?'

Keith did not answer.

'What he doing with half his dick out of his pants anyway, you weren't...'

Keith took another sip of his whisky. 'You know me well Sam, I ain't into blokes.'

Sam was curious, confused, but still scared.

'So what, you killed him and checked if he had a boner or something?'

'No Sam, that's not what happened!' Keith finally got up

from his chair and passed his hand on his gray hair. 'Shall I tell you the sanitised version, or you prefer the brutal, honest one?'

'Humour me.' Sam's manner was becoming less friendly and more suspicious.

'Ok, I lied.'

Sam got on his right knee first before, slowly but steadily getting on his feet. He couldn't afford any sudden moves that would make Keith react. Now, as never in his life, before he not only didn't trust Keith, he was terrified of him.

'It was Van. Van killed 'im.' Keith finally let out.

'V-Van? My Van?'

Keith drew a deep, long breath. 'It seems she wasn't only your Van, I'm afraid,' he cocked his head towards Callum, who seemed to be getting more attention dead than he ever got in life. 'Hence the peeping willy.'

Sam was getting more agitated now, 'Keith, what the fuck is goin' on 'ere?' Sam's South East London drawl was becoming more apparent.

Keith held his hands up, 'nowt to do wi'me matey. Looks like she got the 'umps 'cos you was messing around wi'the ladies.'

Keith was sitting on the edge of the desk now, looking Sam straight in the eyes, something he'd never dare to do as recently as that afternoon. 'She was well pissed off, she was, Van.'

Sam tried to keep a cool head. *How much does Keith know?* He was calculating the distance between where he was and the door, some six feet away. *Probably everything now.* Sam had to think fast. He was younger than Keith and could probably outfight him and if anything, outrun his as well.

'And she *knifed* him? I don't get it.'

'I dunno what happened here, but it seems he was keepin' tabs on ya, and she was shaggin'im at the same time, fella.'

'Keeping tabs?' Sam was more concerned about the spying bit than the fact his Vanessa was fucking an old rival.

'Yeah,' Keith drew another long breath as he uttered the word, 'tabs. As in spying while you was banging me Louise, you treacherous cunt.'

119

The two men kept their distance. Sam was almost shitting himself as he sensed he was in a vulnerable position in the office. His desk was too much of an obstacle to the door. Keith's desk from which he still hadn't moved was closest to any escape route. Unless you count the window behind Sam's chair that led to Lee High road. Two floors below.

Keith remained calm, calculating, even – his usual self. That's what scared Sam the most.

He probably has a weapon ready, he thought. Sam's fear. Keith's advantage.

'Mate, Lou was never... I mean, I wasn't the only one Keith, believe me.' Whether Keith believed that or not was beside the point. Sam needed to buy some time.

'So that gave you the right to bang 'er, right?' Keith responded flat and monotone. 'There are lines you must never cross, Sam.'

'I won't say I regret it, you know me well, but sometimes...,' Sam was almost pleading, 'we just think with our dicks. I'm sure if it were the other way round,' Sam could feel the sweat around his neck, 'you'd probably do it as well...'

'I may be a crook, a bit of a thug even, but I do 'ave a sense of loyalty Sam. At least towards you, I had.'

A cold silence filled the room. Keith just had to seize the perfect moment. Sam probably just needed two seconds and shitloads of luck.

'But you're right Sam.' He slammed the glass on his desk.

'Right...' Sam followed as Keith stood and straightened up, 'about what?'

'You know,' Keith cocked his head and nodded sideways, a smirk slowly drawing on his face, 'the other way round thing.'

'What do you mean?'

'As I said just now Sam, Van was not yours exclusively. And I'll tell you this much,' Keith took a small, cautious yet confident step forward, 'she has to have the firmest ass I've ever had the luck to squeeze,' he lifted his middle finger towards his nose, 'Hmm, I still have her smell on me fingers mate. She so loved it, I tell ya, whatever happens between us now, it was fucking worth it.'

'You trying to wind me up, right?'

'You don't get it, innit? I. Fucked. Your. Wife. About two hours ago, if you need to know.'

Sam stood his ground. Whether Keith was lying or not, he could not fall into provocations – that's probably what Keith wanted. Sam still needed to be ahead of the game. It was tragic that this successful partnership should end like this, he thought.

That fucking tart.

It was time now for a swift exercise in damage limitation.

'And you know the beauty of it all, Sam?' Keith interrupted Sam's thinking and took another step towards him. 'She was the one what asked me to fuck her.'

It happened so fast, it was hard to determine who made the first move.

No shots were fired, it wasn't necessary. As soon as Sam saw Keith, who was within two feet of his desk, attempting to draw, he simply kicked it from the drawers' cabinet, exacting a hollow blow on Keith's abdomen. That gave Sam the momentum and the precious half a second to ram a straight punch to the face, leaving Keith off-balance with the unfortunate consequence that he fell back and hit his head on the edge of his own desk.

A sickening, dry thud made sure Keith would be joining the queue to his final weighing in by the time he met the floor.

Sam stepped towards the body of his old fixer, the man who'd saved his financial ass so many times, who'd also start negotiations with any rival, or client for that matter, softening the conditions in his favour. The man who from time immemorial had looked up at him as the older brotherly role model. The man he betrayed for a pound of pubic flesh.

'I'm sorry it ended like this me 'ol mate,' Sam knelt and like he did with Callum Doherty moments earlier, put his fingers around his jugular area. 'I really am,' he was even starting to choke up a little.

He walked towards Keith's desk and saw his bottle of fine

malt. There was no point arguing Keith's petulance in nicking a dram without permission. He simply grabbed it by the neck and allowed himself a generous gulp.

'Argh!' he gasped as the fiery nectar traveled down his throat.

Sam now had two bodies that needed disposing of. In addition, there were the bloodstains where both Keith and Callum laid. To make matters worse, the only person he could trust to clear up this mess was lying dead in front of him. This was definitely not a good night for Sam.

He also had to see how to break the news to Louise. Vanessa's allowance increase was now the least of his problems.

'A fine mess you got y'self into luv.'

Sam hadn't noticed when Vanessa walked into the office. He turned around and saw her under the door's arch.

'Look, Van,' was all he was able to utter. 'It was an accident. I didn't mean to kill 'im. I was trying to get out of his way,' he said in a nervous stutter, 'he was gonna kill me, you know.'

She frowned at him and pouted. 'Oh... abandoning ship like a rat?'

Sam ignored the remark. 'You had Cal spying on me?'

'He was pretty good at it,' she still didn't move from under the door frame. 'Mind you, he was a decent fuck as well.'

'If you were so pissed off at me, why didn't you say so? Look, it was nothing serious, Lou was always way into me and...' Sam was sitting at Keith's desk swirling the bottle of whisky. He was feeling his empire imploding before his eyes.

'I mean... with my best friend?' Vanessa was still not on the verge of tears, but her words sounded bitter and almost broken.

'I know. And I'm sorry my lovie.'

'Fuckin'ell you sorry, you old piece of shit!' She shouted back.

Sam sat quietly. Vanessa was a lost cause. He slowly started lowering his hand to his pocket.

'... and Keith, he was like your younger brother... he fucking idolised you, Sam.'

Sam took another swig from the bottle. His other hand was on the trigger. 'Van, let me make it up to you. Look, we can sort this out...'

'Yeah, what about your bitch, gonna leave her behind?'

'C'mon Van... she means nothing, you know. Anyway, look at Callum, you're deep in this shit as much as I am,' Sam was desperate. Vanessa had just become another liability. They'd had a good few years together, but his ass held higher priority right now than his marriage. 'I love you, babe, don't leave me.'

'Go fuck yourself, Sam,' she bawled back as she stormed out the office.

Sam got up and started chasing after her. One more body would hardly make a difference now. By the time he cleared the door to his office, he was greeted by two armed officers.

At least, he didn't have to worry about clearing the bodies.

A soft but warm breeze blew through the narrow stretches of Papadiamanti Street. The cobbled surface burned like incandescent charcoals on the soles. Fanakis Taverna could not have appeared any sooner.

It was hard to tell where the Taverna's blue awning blended with Skianthos' cloudless blue sky. Unfortunately, it hardly offered any shady respite from the punishing Sporades sunshine. The suffocating heat underneath made it uncomfortable for sitting, let alone drinking.

Vanessa decided it would be best go inside. It had just turned a quarter past one and she was still twenty minutes early. She had definitely earned her cold bottle of *Mythos*.

Inside was not that much cooler, just less hot and humid. After gulping almost half the bottle in one breath, Vanessa perused the menu – octopus salad, a seafood platter or barbequed monkfish. Probably all three?

'Gosh, you beat me to it, Van,' a familiar voice interrupted her perusing. 'I also thought I'd get here early and have me a cheeky beer before meeting you.'

'Seems we both had the same idea,' Vanessa laughed as she

turned to greet her friend with the obligatory two kisses, in true Mediterranean fashion.

'So glad you finally made it.'

'In a long winded fashion, but yes, here I am.'

'One cannot take risks, I guess.' Vanessa nodded towards an empty table in the darkest corner of the Taverna. 'Seems cooler back there... and more intimate.'

They both headed to the table, menus in hand, not before asking for another couple of *Mythos*.

'By the way, the brown hair really suits you, Van.'

'Thanks, sweetie,' Vanessa returned the compliment winking her right eye, 'and you've picked up a bit of a tan.'

They both smiled.

'You do look more relaxed.'

'Oh definitely,' there was a serene tone to Vanessa's reply, 'At least Sam won't be a nuisance for some time. Twenty-five years, with parole after fifteen if he's well-behaved and still alive.'

Sam's three legitimate businesses had been in Vanessa's name for many years and she managed to launder most of his ill-gained liquid assets before setting him up. Because of that – and inside help from the Met Police anti-fraud department, there could be no way of tracing them back to Sam. The Old Bill seized the rest of his assets. Vanessa didn't care; that was the deal she made with them to get Sam detained and her out of the picture. Callum's death was pinned on Keith, who of course was unable to protest his innocence. Collateral damage, they call it?

'I'm sorry I had to neglect you during the trial despite all your help,' Vanessa said with genuine contrition in her voice.

'Don't worry. I lived. Besides, you had to sound the distraught wife and all.'

'I know. At times, I almost believed it.'

'You poor thing...'

'Better the devil you know, right?' Vanessa whispered as their hands met on the table, caressing tenderly. 'You know I love you.'

'Me too, my little kitten. I can't wait to get my hands on you, baby. It's been far too long.'

'I know. But first, let's eat.'

Vanessa then grabbed Louise by her face, pulled her towards the centre of the table and they both locked into a viciously tender kiss.

NO EASY ANSWER

She danced a while and drank some wine
before she rolled her eyes at me
I picked them up and I rolled them back,
and then we swam into the sea

She's Alright - Stereophonics

Oh shit! Holy, bloody, mother fucking shit!

I lay helplessly on the bed, the pointy end of a thick, sharp bit drilling through my skull!

The pounding continues, the throbbing is relentless, like a concerto of mad drummers banging away on a ritualistic death beat. I try opening my eyes, but the puncturing pressure against my skull is unbearable.

I don't wanna die like this!

Slowly, the high-pitched, drilling noise becomes faint, although the pain inside my head remains. I suddenly feel at ease. I open my eyes and an eerie silence takes over.

I am dead. Finally.

Thank God.

Well, I think so. Or...

Fuck, no. I am very much alive.

Painfully alive.

At the time, it seemed like the perfect idea – a weekend break, away from everyone. I could have gone local, maybe Eastbourne, Brighton, even venture further west to Portsmouth or Bath. However, the more I thought about it, the less appealing they felt.

I had two weeks left to submit my article, and I had done fuck all! The approaching deadline felt as welcoming as a bailiff's visit.

As a freelance travel writer, my articles help pay my mortgage, petrol for my car, food for the refrigerator – and subsequently, dinner table – and those little indulgences I like to allow myself once in awhile.

Unfortunately, not all travel writers lead a glamorous life peppered with high-end luxury. I can't remember the last time I travelled first class or stayed at a five-star hotel, let alone sipping margaritas, mojitos or any exotic sounding cocktail at the side of an infinity pool while contemplating and oozing over bikini-clad beauties – I could probably remember, at a push, the last three star or budget hostel.

I cannot feel a hole or anything to indicate my brains are spilling out, although that is exactly how I feel. Not too sure if being alive is worth all this pain.

Anyway, good to know there's no mad killer in the vicinity attempting to perform a lobotomy without the anaesthetic.

Same effect nevertheless.

More than pins and needles, I feel I've nails and daggers in my head!

Having finally figured out, not so much *who* I am but more around the lines of where I am, why I am here, I'm wondering why I have what looks like two large lumps lying at each side of me beneath the covers.

Shit, my head is killing me. Christ almighty, even opening my eyes hurts.

Right, the bulging shapes under the duvet.

Dear God, please don't let them be two blokes... and for what it's worth now, please let them be alive...

Most of the articles I write are experiences I actually have to pay for – I did mention I am a freelancer – therefore, I need to go from publication to publication, extolling the virtues of my write-ups. Now you see my predicament.

This particular website I regularly contribute to, however, made me a very attractive offer. I had to write about a holiday that could capture not only the reader's imagination but also the advertisers' interest. It had to be something unusual, something hardly anyone had experienced. Yeah, easy shit!

Initially, I'd have to finance it myself, and only if they thought the story was worth publishing would they reimburse my expenses, besides paying me handsomely. Staying home obviously defeated the purpose of this project.

I did mention I'm a *travel* writer.

So, in pursuit of exotic adventures, I chose a destination within easy reach and inside my paltry budget. A wheelie bag with a few essentials for an autumnal weekend out and a rucksack for my laptop and other writing essentials were my possessions for this trip.

It's slowing down now, thank God.

The room, that is.

Right, I'm awake... that means ... I am alive, which is always a good thing.

My head...

Oh yes... under the covers. The two shapes.

I'm scared to look.

'Hmm...'

A sound.

The voice seems rather high-pitched and human. And very alive.

Encouraging.

It's coming from my left side though. What's to my right then? There's no sound coming from that body – shit, why did I say that!

Let's peep under the sheets.

Holy fucking shit!

Two women – and they're breathing.

Ok, at least I haven't killed anyone.

I gently lower the sheet and duvet.

No ... I need to see this again...

They *are* completely naked – all fucking two of them.

In bed. *My* bed.

Fuck! Just once more...

Yep, they are definitely women.

And they are still naked.

'So you've been in Madrid before?'

'Yes, a few times,' I replied between bites of my chicken wrap and gulps of the red *Tempranillo* wine I chose to accompany it. 'And you were in London for business, leisure?'

'A bit of both,' she replied in a very strong Spanish accent. 'By the way, I am Elena, and you are...?'

'Glen,' I said trying not to lodge the never-ending chewed piece of chicken I'd been trying to swallow since we started this conversation, 'Glen Taylor.'

'And you're going to Madrid for work?'

'Well sort of...' I tried stretching the momentum, hoping she would ask what my line of work was. As a freelance writer, I always embrace the chance to promote myself.

She didn't ask.

Shit, what day is it?

I need to look at these birds again. Hmm... long, dark hair, fair skin, and reasonable figures. The one on my left has a very nice ass by the way.

The one to the right has long hair as well; curly, black as night, unruly. Not a bad figure as far as my hungover eyes can make out. She's got an ass but can't make out how nice it is or not.

Well, under these circumstances most asses look good.

I draw the sheets all the way out until we're all uncovered. I gently and carefully climb over the woman on my right to get out the bed.

I kneel down and check her face.

My God!

What the hell is *she* doing here?

Of course, I bit into the trap. 'Some research, visit a friend, get some inspiration for a project I'm working on.' This must *surely* whet her appetite.

It didn't.

Elena playfully flicked her black curls, offering me a smile that at times looked sensual, at times inconsequential, but mostly vague.

Probably in her mid-thirties or thereabouts, Elena's face exuded juvenile mischief, but at the same time contained a mature and sophisticated air. The small freckles on her upper cheekbones just added more mystery.

Elena's green eyes simply stared at me, her blank expression giving away close to nothing as to whether she was interested or not in what I did for a living. I hate these silly games.

'Your work sounds interesting.'

Shit, she looks good naked!

If only I could remember how she got here... and when?

And for that matter, this other one here.

Let's pull back the covers and get out. I'm still not prepared to scare the shit out of either of them.

This other one here is almost exposed. If only I could see her face properly, the bloody hair's all over the place.

As I reach the other side of the bed, she turned inwards.

Damn it!

I can't help but contemplate.

Hell, she looks good!

I fight the urge to follow the curves of her hips with my fingers. *And shit, what an ass!*

Now, if only I could see her face...

Yeah, that's great now. Curl up and cuddle the damn pillow, now I really can't see shit!

Still, she has a nice ass...

I tried to keep up with Elena's pace as we walked towards passport control. I couldn't stop marveling at how her cream denims sensually contoured her slightly full thighs, while a loose fitting pastel blue linen blouse strategically concealed her *derriere*, which would have looked just as hot tucked inside her jeans as it did overflowing.

Before we landed, I scribbled my mobile number on the back of one of my business cards. After finally catching up with Elena as we approached the immigration booths, I handed it over to her.

She looked at the card, flicked it over, and twitched her lips as she noticed my number scribbled on the back, smiled again, and put the card inside her handbag. Unfortunately, she didn't reciprocate, pretty much negating any hope of future contact.

'Look, I have to rush,' was all she added, 'you enjoy yourself and good luck with your project.'

'Hey, feel free to call, maybe you can tell me a few things I need to know about Madrid,' my sentence losing intensity as I noticed her lack of interest.

She smiled and shrugged her shoulders before reaching the immigration officer. 'I think you will discover things yourself.'

The *coup de grace* to my ego.

I had to let someone go ahead in front of me while I searched for my passport. By the time I found it and advanced the queue, Elena was gone.

Still can't recognise the face. I'll go draw the blinds a bit to get some light in.

It's cloudy outside, but enough light seeps through the little gap

Blimey! Such a mess of clothes on the floor. What the fuck went on in here?

Ok. There are my trousers. And my socks.

Black knickers? One brown shoe?

Ah, there's the other one. That over there... looks like a dress.

Fuck, a bra. Definitely, not mine.

Where did the last few hours of my life go?

Towering at an impressive six foot five, and weighing around sixteen stone, Mark Bruford can be intimidating when you first meet him. His deep thunderous voice just adds to it. At 48, he is only six years older than me, but his hard mug gives him a deceivingly older look. His almost white dead-straight hair tightly combed back and ending in a two to three-inch ponytail, contrasts with the thin mousy brown padlock goatee on his tanned face. His steely grey eyes hardly invite bullshit. A very small diamond encrusted stud adds a touch of glamour to his left earlobe.

It is Mark alright – my old drinking buddy and trouble seeking mate of blazing and blasting years, alas, all long gone.

As soon as I walk out of the turnstiles at Atocha station, he holds out his beefy hands as a loving father ready to embrace a returning son.

'Ah, my dear old Gleneth, how bloody good to see you!' he barks.

I last saw him four years ago when he was still living near me in Southeast London. 'Just look at you, you even look respectable now!'

Just past midnight, Atocha was almost deserted, bar a few tramps, the odd zonked out youths still trying to work out what leg they should put forward first, and the odd lone figures ambling aimlessly across the main concourse.

Mark took my wheelie and we left the station.

As we walked past throes of party revellers through Paseo del Prado towards my hotel, Mark was telling me about his new life in Madrid.

'So, your big sister still hates me, Gleneth?'

'Hate you... well, that's a bit of a big word,' I answered uncomfortably as I avoided stepping on some dog shit littered on the pavement. 'She ... she just doesn't want me near you, that's all.'

'Tragic to hear,' his slight sarcasm bursts out in a thunderous laugh.

'It probably explains why you declined my hospitality then.'

'Mark, I told you already, this is supposed to be a work-related trip. Can you imagine me getting anything done with you around me?'

'I am deeply offended, you know – fuck, look at *that* bird man!'

I looked, she was ok, but, I'd seen better. 'Someone's desperate.'

'Anyway, Sophie always has her little brother's best interest at heart.'

I elbowed him in his ribs. 'Look, I hear there's a cool whisky bar at my hotel. Fancy a drink before I crash out – if you're ok for time?'

He gave me a studious look. 'As if that should bother you, I ... I am ok for *one* drink pal.'

I lean on the side of the larger of the two windows and look towards the bed. My headache seems to be ebbing away slowly, but trying to tie up the events that led up to this, is bringing on a different kind of pain.

Why can I not remember anything?

Shit! Mark.

We *did* meet last night. What happened there?

I'm now starting to feel a bit sick.

Wardrobe!

Yes, these are still my clothes.

Now, the safe.

Strangely enough, I can still remember the code. All my stuff are still the way I vaguely remember putting them – wallet, passport, some loose notes, flight itinerary, house keys...

Oh, shit!

Mark did indeed leave after just one drink. I was in my room by around two am. As we enjoyed a single malt each, he told me of his new life in Madrid, working as an English teacher for executives and playing the drums in a blues band of geriatric farts at rooftop bars in the evenings.

He now lives with his current girlfriend, a feisty Basque with as bad an attitude as his, according to him.

'Ours is a match lovingly brewed in hell,' Mark explained.

Mark left an estranged wife and two teenage boys back in London, in addition to a police caution after pulverizing an ex-colleague's nose following the discovery that he and Mark's wife were having an affair. This in part explains Sophie's aversion towards him.

With Mark's beefy hands, you can only imagine what sort of damage his knuckles can inflict. My being on much better terms with him, we agreed to meet up the next afternoon for a proper night out, as he had no gigs planned.

My mobile's not here.

Where could I have left the fucking thing now?

Shit, now one of them is even snoring! I just hope I didn't make any stupid calls or send embarrassing messages.

Two naked women fast asleep in my bed, a headache from hell, short-term memory loss, and a missing mobile phone.

Unless I'm in some sort of weird parallel world, this shit doesn't look good.

Next morning, after a traditional Spanish breakfast at a café opposite the hotel, I went on the prowl for something exciting to discover and subsequently write on Madrid, clueless on how to start my research and nobody with whom to share or even discuss my ideas.

Elena came to mind.

What a bloody fool I'd been, trying to flirt with a fellow passenger I had only just met. She was pretty stunning, what could I do?

I could have sat next to a fat, sweaty old fart last night. That would have made my life so much easier.

Trying to focus on my task ahead, I resorted to my classical 1-2-3-4 routing to see where I ended up. That is taking the first street left, then second right, third left again, and finally fourth right. Having started on Calle Moratín, near my hotel, I ended in Calle Valencia, in the Lavapiés neighbourhood.

Cosmopolitan, bohemian, somewhat edgy, *Lavapiés* certainly held a dark and rough appeal. However, I couldn't find anything remotely esoteric or sinister. Something I could write about that would make people grab their rucksack and head straight there. I was probably searching too eagerly.

I went into a bar and ordered a beer.

From *Lavapiés* I wandered off to *La Latina*. From there, and a couple of beers later, I end up in Puerta de Toledo before taking the metro back to my hotel. My greatest find so far was the inability to get Elena out of my head.

I went into another bar.

As I pick up my trousers, lying shapelessly on the floor, I feel something slightly heavy in one of the pockets.

Here you are. My phone! Relief.

I straighten it and remove the phone from the pocket.

This is a fucking Blackberry.

Now, how did this end up inside my pocket? Where is my

phone?

And who in their right fucking mind uses a Blackberry nowadays!

Ok, focus. There is enough light in here. Calm the fuck down, and look properly.

Aha! What's that under the bed?

There's a square black something underneath. Now, slow and quiet, still don't want to wake them.

Damn it.

Now every fucking bone in me is creaking!

Come on, just a little further. *Yes.* Got it. Now slide the little fucker back to daddy.

My phone. Panic over.

For now.

Right. An Iphone in one hand and a Blackberry in the other, two naked women still in my bed... this is the kind of shit that gets you in trouble.

What the fuck could have possibly gone wrong?

Fuck!

I too am completely naked.

The first day almost over, and I've achieved fuck all. This was promising to be one write-off of a trip. Well, at least catching up with an old friend should save the night.

Dressed in his customary black, Mark sat on the equally black chaise-longue propped opposite the reception desk. Arms folded, stone-faced, tinted shades, some kind of ethnic necklace offering a colourful contrast to his all-black attire, Mark resembled more a mad testosterone-filled gangster itching for a fight than the gregarious, larger than life character readying for a drink.

'I've got some good and some bad news mate,' he said solemnly as he stood to greet me.

'What's wrong now?'

'Well, the good news is I'm taking you to one wicked rooftop bar near *Sol*. The views of Madrid are spectacular, the birds are fucking hot, and the booze is top class – expensive, but definitely worth every Euro.'

'... and the bad news?' I asked, thinking that having said that the place was expensive was tragic enough.

'Ainhoa, my girlfriend, is joining us.' His cavernous voice suddenly lacked the thunderous impact it usually has. 'Sadly, I must behave myself.'

'Oh well, shit happens I guess.'

'You know what women are like,' he tucked his hands in his pockets as we walked out the hotel. 'Overbearing, possessive, well, pain in the asses, basically. Anyway... she's curious to see if all the horror stories I told about you are true.'

'And you still wonder why Sophie has this *thing* against you?'

Mark continued, ignoring my remark as we walked towards Sol, 'First though, let's head to a little place I know, just ten minutes from here, discuss your project while we have a quick drink. We'll catch up with her at the hotel.'

I talked him through the project, however, in the end I realised I would have probably gained better feedback and recommendations from my local butcher.

I could almost hear Sophie's perennial *I told you so* and *only a gullible moron would seek advice from Mark Bruford.*

A couple of glasses of beer and a meagre saucer of inedible tapas later, we headed off to the *Innside Roof Terrace* atop the former *Hotel Suecia.*

Ainhoa was already waiting for us at the reception.

After the usual ritual of greetings, introductions, the two kisses, we took the lift up to the Terrace.

I immediately warmed up to this rooftop terrace. It was past eight o'clock and not a single cloud in the sky. A very classy venue this was, indeed. The place was relatively full but not mega-packed. You could still hear yourself think, which is always a good thing.

Everyone seemed relaxed. Men looked handsome, in a very laidback way. Women looked classy without much effort.

Ainhoa, on the other hand, was stunning – and I mean, obscenely, shamelessly, and unapologetically hot. Ok, she was my friend's girlfriend but it still didn't alter the fact that under different circumstances, I would happily bury myself between her thighs.

The soft blue, red, purple and green spotlights scattered around the terrace offered a relaxed and slightly decadent hue to the place as the dying sunlight gave way to the night.

Ainhoa's hair seemed dark brown at times, then black, depending on what light shone on her. It was dead straight and cascaded over her shoulders, softly caressing her golden-tanned skin. Perfectly plucked eyebrows magnified her grey quartz-like eyes that just invited trouble. High cheekbones on an oval face, pointed chin that begged for a bite on which a pouty mouth that conjured mischief rested, was hard to ignore.

Suddenly, her joining us for the night did not seem a bad idea.

I discretely scanned her figure while we searched for a table, loungers, or anywhere to settle. She was on the slim side but well curved. A light blue cotton dress with white flower patterns ending perilously around mid-thighs perfectly contoured her figure.

Heart attack inducing.

By ten thirty, we had downed three rounds of cocktails – pretty much depleting my booze budget for this trip among other things.

At that point, Mark was quite drunk. I was relatively tipsy, but still in control. Ainhoa was the only one still holding her drink well but there was no way of shutting her up – not that I minded nor cared. My dirty mind was doing overtime.

If I couldn't provide a meaningful article for this client, at least I would allow my eyes to feast on this hot Basque beauty.

'Guys, I think we need a refill,' I announced.

As I stood from our loungers, the world suddenly started spinning at inconceivable speed. For a brief couple of seconds, Madrid suddenly flipped upside-down. I almost stumbled but caught my balance immediately.

'Please don't embarrass us here,' Ainhoa held out a hand just in case. We both laughed. Mark was already in planet Zonk.

Once the world, including the Spanish capital, had returned to its rightful axis, I took a leap of faith and headed to the bar.

As I stood, I glanced over the railings and admired Madrid in all its splendour – the former post-office building, the buzzing *Gran Via*, the white neo-classical rooftops.

I was sure this city had some mischief hidden within it. I was still too blind to discover it.

As well as almost too drunk.

'Ay, Dios mio... mi cabeza...' (A*h, my God ... my head...*) a raspy voice grunts. It's the one on the right side of the bed.

I timidly walked towards her.

She attempts to sit up but that effort proves extremely taxing.

I am now standing before her.

'Ostias,' she grunts and slowly tilts her head up towards my face.

Of course, I am still naked and well, under the circumstances, I guess such a sight all of a sudden can cause surprise. For the right or wrong reasons.

I lower myself and level with her face.

She opens her mouth to say something but simply stares at me, not quite seeming to register my presence. She closes her eyes and let out a whispery breath. 'Mierda,' she sighs.

Shit.

From the bar, I could still see Ainhoa leaning against the balcony, while Mark sat, drink miraculously still in hand, almost in a catatonic state. Her raw, almost intimidating sex appeal, even from where I was standing, was simply mesmerising. I was now studying her unapologetically. From face to cleavage, breasts to waist, ass to legs, no shame, basic decency chucked out the window. Scenes from *The Mask* film suddenly came to mind.

'Caballero!' the murmur turned into a bark. It was the barman.

'Sí, disculpe,' I turned towards him, my mind joining a few seconds later. I ordered another round.

Mark was still sitting, and it seemed he was holding some sort of conversation with an imaginary listener, as Ainhoa, still leaning against the glass balcony, elbows resting on the steel railings, attentively ignored him.

I simply stood transfixed, glued to her silhouette, the slight breeze that suddenly picked up gently blowing against her hair. All of a sudden, she slowly turned towards Mark as if to acknowledge whatever he was saying, then again, turned back towards the Madrid skyline.

It could have been my imagination, or probably a touch of guilt, but I could have sworn she stole a quick glimpse towards me.

The barman summoned me back to reality again. I turned to see our drinks lined up before me and after almost choking when I saw the eye-wateringly extortionate bill, I dug into my back pocket to get out my wallet.

'Tu amigo carga un pedo que te cagas!' *Your friend is as drunk as a skunk.*

Ainhoa almost scared the shit out of me. How did she get here so fast? Or had time simply stopped for me?

'Hey, you here!' I noticed a slight slur in my voice.

'That is the thing with Mark,' she continued, 'sometimes he is like a bottomless pit when he drinks.'

'Ah, is that so?' As if I'd never drunk with him back home.

'Yeah,' she sighed slightly annoyed, 'but at least he doesn't get violent or loud and stupid. He just falls asleep.'

'Well, better that way, right?'

'Have you tried moving Mark's dead weight when he is asleep?'

I left it at that.

'Erm, you didn't need to come over,' I changed the subject. 'I could manage ok with the drinks.'

'I didn't come to help you, *cabroncete.*' Her eyes twinkled with mischief as she lowered her face just slightly.

'No? Then, why?'

'Well, because you were looking at my ass,' Ainhoa said bluntly, with a soft hiss that carried a subtle threat yet at the same time sounded mischievously sexy.

'What?' Her bluntness hardly gave me any chance to work up a credible defence, 'where... what... you talking about?'

Ainhoa leaned on me, fixing her gaze. She squinted, smiled, and nodded her head sideways; I felt a cold sweat around my neck. However, I held my ground.

I felt like a kid who'd just been caught stealing his mom's change from her purse, 'I swear it's not like that.' I tried sounding as composed as the situation allowed, and as clear as the alcohol in my system permitted, 'besides, you are Mark's girlfriend.'

'Yes, of course.'

Ainhoa then grabbed one of the drinks. 'Now stop staring at my ass, and let's get back to Mark.'

'What are you doing naked like that?'

'This is my room,' I blurt out as if I have to justify my lack of clothing in my room. 'How did you end up in here?'

Elena takes her time to reply. Whether, like me, she is trying to register her surroundings, or she feels I've just asked the stupidest of questions, I cannot tell.

'Are you being funny or what?'

'Do I look funny?' I realise too late it's probably not the best choice of words.

Of course, she doesn't reply.

Back at our loungers, Mark grabbed me by the arm, almost making me spill the drink I was carrying.

'Me 'ol mate Gleneth,' he slurred his words, 'how good to have ya here me old boy...'

'Yeah, it's good to see you at last you big fucker.'

I stole a quick glance at Ainhoa, who was toying with her drink, poker-faced. She looked over the terrace into the now almost dark Madrid skyline.

Talk about anticlimax. No ideas for a meaningful article, in addition to the prospect of no reimbursement for this trip; my friend plastered beyond repair; the uncomfortable company of a fiercely beautiful woman who looked as reassuring as a schizophrenic monkey with a razor blade.

Not to mention my unashamed desire to shag her.

'I think we must go now,' Ainhoa finally broke her silence.

She stood and turned towards me. Unsurprisingly, she seemed more beautiful. Dangerously beautiful. 'I'm sorry that your friend has not been very good company.'

'I thought he held his drink much better.' I really did think so.

'There are many things he *used* to hold much better.'

I wasn't sure what to read into that. 'It's been nice meeting you, anyway.'

'I know,' Ainhoa turned to me, 'all you've done is stare at my ass and legs all night.'

I stood and took the two steps towards where she was standing, looking towards the former post office building, both hands firmly on the railing, my heart pounding nervously. 'You can't fault me for having good taste.'

There were only two possible outcomes, and I was prepared for the slapped face.

Neither one happened.

'Are you staying here for another drink or will you help me stop a taxi so we can go home?' More than a question, it sounded like an order.

I gulped down my cocktail, the sudden rush of fierce spirit hitting my brains almost immediately.

'Yep. Let's go downstairs. You'll definitely need some help to get this big baby home.'

Fortunately, there was still enough life in Mark to spare us the blushes of having to carry him across the bar and into the lift.

Mark and Ainhoa walked ahead, clumsily clinging to each other. She was right about one thing. I couldn't stop staring at her ass.

'What time is it?'

First sensible question since I woke up.

I notice a flickering red light coming from a clock on the bedside table at the other side of the bed. I walk towards it and turn to see the screen.

It reads 11.37.

I reply as I return to her side of the bed.

'Mierda!' she quickly gets out of bed and hardly bothers to cover herself; not that I really care.

'My shift starts at twelve.'

'Shift? Where do you need to be?'

'Are you stupid or what?' she barks back.

I return a stupid look, reinforcing her remark.

'I work in this hotel, don't you remember?'

Slowly, and very scarily, things are starting to unravel.

Booze.

Taxi.

Bar.

Shower.

Fuck! Ainhoa!

We arrived at Mark and Ainhoa's flat in *Calle de Caracas* in the *Alonso Martinez* area of Madrid. In my state and in the darkness, I couldn't really make out much of the building, but it seemed like a handsomely appointed neo-classic structure.

I got off to help Mark out while Ainhoa spoke to the cab driver.

'C'mon pal,' I whispered to Mark, 'I thought you were much stronger than this.'

'Mate, me days of drinking you under the table are lo-o-ong go-o-one,' he replies with a slur and a lazy laugh. 'Where's me bird?'

'Paying the cab driver.'

'Lovely, ain't she?'

Wouldn't you fucking know?

Ainhoa finally joined us at the entrance. 'Glen, I'll take over from here. Thank you for helping me. The taxi is waiting.'

'No need to mention.' I replied with a hint of resignation, 'Erm, just be careful with him.' I started walking towards the cab.

Ainhoa turned round while precariously maintaining Mark's balance. 'You get inside the taxi and don't go nowhere,' she barks in her thick Spanish accent with an authority I dared not to question. 'I still have to pay the man.'

'I thought you were...' Why was I even bothering! 'Look, I can just...'

'Glen,' she cut me before I could continue, '... just shut up and wait for me to come down.'

Me, argue with a Basque woman?

Suddenly my headache returns fivefold.

Ainhoa.

Just to reconfirm my stupidity I go back to the other side of the bed. I pull back the sheet.

Fuck. It's her.

And now she's fucking snoring too...

I gently cover her again.

'What is that –' Elena says as she turns following my moves. 'Me cago en la...'

I look up to Elena and shrug. What the hell can I say?

Never in my wildest dreams. Ainhoa, in my bed. In all her deranged, dangerous and crazy beauty. And fucking naked.

I don't even notice Elena anymore.

As naked and gorgeous as she is.

Ainhoa returned within five minutes and jumped in the back seat next to me.

'Gracias' she thanked the driver for waiting, the idle sound of the diesel engine almost lulling me to sleep.

'So Glen, where is your hotel?'

'Hey, you didn't need to, my Spanish is good enough, I could have got there without help,' I replied.

'I think your Spanish is shit, so you need help,' I started to find her insane behaviour rather sexy at this stage. 'Anyway, I need help with this,' she said as she produced an interestingly intricately carved bottle.

'What is that?'

'Patxarán,' she replies with a mischievous grin. 'I only hope you hold longer than Mark does.'

We alighted at Paseo del Prado at the end of *Calle de Moratín* and walked the twenty yards or so to my hotel. I took a swig of that wretched Patxarán and still wondered how I was still standing.

Ainhoa grabbed my hand as we walked the final stretch before reaching the hotel's entrance. I felt a mixture of fear, elation, adventure, and guilt.

This has to be the stupidest thing I've done in my entire life.

The whisky bar opposite the hotel's foyer was unusually quiet with all of three or four punters almost doubled over by the time we arrived.

'Why don't we go straight to your room and finish off the Patxarán?'

'I can't just walk past the reception with you in hand, like that?' I explained, startled by her bluntness, 'that receptionist knows I am on my own.'

'Ok, then get me a *cubata*,' Ainhoa agreed as a sensible compromise, 'tell him to load it!' It was the least I'd expect to hear from someone carrying a bottle of Patxarán in her handbag.

Soft, jazzy background music was playing away as we claimed a corner table with two low but firm cushions as seats.

The waiter, a tall black figure with a severe look came over and placed two tumblers half-filled with ice and proceeded to pour our choices of spirits; an 18-year White Label for me, and a Pampero rum for Ainhoa. Once completed, he brought a bottled-water and a can of coke while asking my room number.

I mixed my whisky and water and gave it a gentle stir with my finger. Then, I gulped down a generous sip buying some time to collect my thoughts.

'You seem nervous,' Ainhoa said, placing her glass on the table and playfully caressing my fingers.

'Well, what do you expect, you bloody nutcase!'

'Ah, don't worry, Mark will still be asleep by the time I get home,' she casually replied.

'Yeah, but,' there I am trying to be sensible for a change, 'he's my mate, you shouldn't be doing this... at least not with me!'

'Don't you like me?'

What a stupid question! Since the rooftop terrace, I'd mentally fucked her seven times over!

'You *are* a fucking nutcase Ainhoa!'

'Yeah,' she calmly fingered her drink as she stared at me, daring me to turn away.

I couldn't.

'That's what Mark likes about me... but you didn't answer my question. Do you like me?'

'C'mon, what makes you think I fancy *you*?'

She squinted and twisted her face sideways, as you do when you are about to admonish a child or threaten to rip someone's testicles off.

'You will fancy me if I say you fancy me, is that clear?' Ainhoa leaned further forward and stopped inches from my face. Then she smiled.

Sophie was right, whichever way you looked at it. Even through his deranged girlfriend, Mark was trouble.

I leaned forward and kissed her.

'Glen, would you care to explain?' Elena nods towards Ainhoa.

'I have no idea how *she* ended up here,' I am as confused and she is.

Elena whispers nervously as she points towards Ainhoa's bulk under the sheets, 'but I need to get out of here. No one can see me in this room.'

I can see her point. However, as I scan around the room, all I see are a couple of knickers scattered about, three women's shoe, Ainhoa's crumpled up dress and my clothes.

As hard as I try, I see no easy answer to all this.

'Aren't you gonna get dressed then?' I ask sheepishly. 'I can't remember much, but I am sure you didn't turn up naked.'

Elena turns and gives me a mean, steely glance. 'Don't just stand there, help me find my clothes.'

I can't help but let out a muffled chuckle.

One round was sufficient, and without further ado, we head up to my room. I steal a nervous glance at the reception bloke as we walk past towards the lift, but he simply tilts his head acknowledging me politely.

Inside the lift, all hell broke loose! Ainhoa grabbed me by my buttocks, pulling me towards her and crashed her lips against mine. For a moment, I thought she'd actually smashed my front teeth. Clearly, I offered no resistance, and gave into her deranged kiss as the lift careered – in all directions, I felt – to the third floor.

Miraculously, I found my room and even more amazingly, I opened the door in one go.

As soon as we got inside and I slammed the door, Ainhoa opened her bag and retrieved the bottle of Patxarán. After giving me enough time to catch my breath, she walked towards where I was standing, clung to my neck and wrapped her legs around me, again, overpowering me with a savage kiss, while still holding the wretched bottle of the Basque's brew from hell.

I have no idea how much time had passed but next thing I remembered, Ainhoa and I were on my bed, busy in our linguistic exploration when suddenly a loud knock on the door stopped us in our tracks.

'You expecting someone?' For the first time, I saw something resembling nervousness in her.

'I...actually, no,' I replied, probably more nervous, and still relatively more sober than Ainhoa, or at least, with a more acute sense of fear than hers.

I motioned for her to keep quiet and for good measure, indicated she hides in the bathroom. After all, I did book as sole occupant.

Once Ainhoa was properly ensconced, I softly tiptoed towards the door and looked through the peephole. A female figure was standing outside holding what seemed like a pad or a notebook.

'Erm...yes?' I finally said.

'Good evening sir,' replied the female voice, 'I am the duty manager and I think you may have left your phone at the bar a short while ago?'

Christ!

I felt for my pocket and noticed I didn't have it on me. 'Just a moment, please,' I quickly walked to the dressing table where I threw my jacket. I checked the pockets, and couldn't find my phone either.

How nice of them. How lucky too.

'Hang on a second,' I cried back as I checked I was in decent shape.

As I opened the door, the night suddenly became that bit more surreal.

'It's you!'

'It seems Madrid has revealed more than I bargained for...'

Elena looked as embarrassed as I was surprised. '*Ostias!* I really don't know what to say, I ...'

'To be honest, I totally understand...' more like, *yeah right bitch!*

'Hey, thanks for finding my phone anyway...' The way things were going, I could ill afford further stupid remarks, 'would you like to come in and join me for a drink at least?'

Shit, was I fucking deranged as well? What was I thinking?

'I'm sorry Mr. Taylor,' she quickly excused herself.

'Glen,' I interject, 'please, call me Glen.'

'Sorry, yes, Glen,' Elena rectified, 'my shift finishes in about half an hour,' she fidgeted with her badge, '...but, if you are still awake,' green eyes widen and lips narrow playfully. 'I have an early shift tomorrow, so, erm, I am staying here for tonight...but only one drink.'

'One it is, then.' This. Is. Not. Happening.

Well, the invitation was there. At least, for the time being, I had...

Shit! Ainhoa.

In the bathroom.

Elena and I both get dressed, after finally finding her uniform, strewn across the room in the most impossible of places.

'So are you going to tell me what exactly happened?'

'Are you telling me you don't remember *anything?*'

'Let's see, what part of 'no' do you not seem to understand?'

'No need to be so pedantic!' Elena barks back.

'Let's see. I came to bring back your mobile,' she tries not to trip while putting on her skirt in haste. That I remember.

'...we recognised each other, we laughed, and you invited me in.' I now remember that, too.

'As I was almost ending my shift, I said I would come back and join you for a drink...'

'Which, by the look of things, you did...yes, continue!'

'I came back, we drank some Patxarán...'

Shit, the brew from hell.

'And after that –' she stopped and turned to me, 'look, are you sure you don't remember or are you just being an idiot?'

'For fuck sake Elena, I've no time for being clever and shit! First, this... lunatic drags me here, leaves my good friend, *her boyfriend,* at home, then you turn up and end up naked in my bed –'

'Not my problem!'

'Well I wouldn't be... look, just tell me what else happened.'

'I'm sorry,' she's finished dressing but looks like shit. 'I

ANT RICHARDS

have to be in the office in, erm,' she looks at her watch. 'Mierda! Two minutes ago!'

She fits on her shoes as she walks towards the door, almost tripping in the process, 'look, we'll have to continue this conversation later. But now, I have to go.'

'Yes, go ahead...' *Yeah, just fuck off.*

The door slams and I'm now left with a deranged, Basque lunatic, still fast asleep on my bed.

As if shit hadn't got any heavier, there is probably an hour or so of my life still missing.

Now I need to try to wake Ainhoa up, get her out of my room, and send her home without arousing Mark's suspicion.

'Hey,' I start patting her on her shoulder, 'wake up you little nutcase...'

She growls something, waves me off with her left hand then turns around. Shit, this is going to be hard work.

Still, what a beautiful ass she's got…

After a few rattles and gentle shakings, Ainhoa finally wakes up.

'Me cago en...'

She suddenly tries to get up but like Elena earlier on, this effort seems to tax her enormously.

She looks at me and nods her head sideways.

'You son of a bitch... you left me in the bathroom!'

I *did*? 'I tried to wake you, but you just didn't move,' I lie, 'and I ... I was too drunk to lift you up.'

She simply gave a spoilt pout and crossed her arms. 'Was that after or before you told me to hide?'

That I don't remember.

'You took so long to get rid of that woman I fell asleep. Did you fuck her as well?'

Did I? For that matter, did I even shag Ainhoa?

Should I ask her?

'Of course, when I woke up, you were fast asleep!'

'So you just slid into the bed, right?'

'No! I floated...' she bawls out, '...*será capullo*!'

Great! Everything seems to be *my* fault now!

'Look Ainhoa, you've gotta get back home fast.' And I need to fly back to London as soon as possible.

She doesn't answer.

'Just be careful, please. The last thing I need is for Mark to find out about last night.'

She simply snorts out, turns her face, and crosses her arms again.

Inside the lift, the trip on the way down feels nauseating. I feel like I have a heavy rock tied to my waist pulling me down, the rest of my body following with an unnatural delay.

As the door opens, the midday light that pierces through the corridor and into the lift slaps me back to reality. I slowly make my way to the reception desk.

In zombie mode, I slowly and laboriously check my room bill, relieved there are no outrageous mini-bar bills or damage charges. The moral cost I carry is sufficient debt to last me a lifetime.

Especially, when I've no idea of what I did or didn't do.

I suppose, with time, memories of what happened in room 271 will slowly return to me. In the meantime, I can only fantasize of what I would have loved to have done last night.

I check the receipt, happy to see a big, fat zero in the balance box.

'My word Gleneth, you do look like shit this morning! Leaving us already?'

Oh crap...

Donned in his customary black attire; sitting on the equally black chaise-longue propped opposite the reception desk. Arms folded, stone-faced, tinted shades, this time no ethnic necklace to contrast his all-black attire, Mark no longer resembles the gregarious party animal ready for a drink but a testosterone mad gangster itching for a fight.

... also by Ant Richards

IN YOUR DREAMS

2000

Carl Manning was still sweating and trembling when he entered the church. This was his last chance – it was either God or the police.

Manning refused to take his friends' calls. As they came in, he pressed the 'end call' button. The text messages he received, at first with a hysterical sense of urgency, soon turned menacing. Manning finally texted back begging forgiveness and saying how unworthy he was of anybody's sympathy and help. Nevertheless, he refused to answer the calls.

The voice messages soon followed. First it was a message threatening to call the police. Next it was a promise to reorganise his face if he refused to pick up. Still, Manning did not answer.

The large, arched wooden door was slightly ajar, and Manning simply pushed a little and entered. The church was empty; the eerie silence and emptiness inside exaggerated the thumping of his steps despite him wearing trainers.

Manning had finally hit rock bottom. The events that culminated in his coming to this church went beyond anything he had done over the past six years, since his problems began.

Halfway down the nave, he turned right and sat at a pew to regain his breath. Reordering his thoughts, well, that was a different story.

Manning was no stranger to the concept of prayer, but he was unable to utter the first word. He was not entirely sure whether he actually wanted to pray. In his opinion, he was beyond repair. He had already caused too much hurt and pain to his family. The lies, empty promises, and colossal debts had taken a huge toll. Gambling addiction was a right bastard. Like alcoholism, drug addiction, and any other kind of habit abuse, it was the closest and dearest that bore the brunt of the pain.

This past week had been difficult. He'd had two interview rejections, had little money left, and was desperate and without hope. A fertile ground to unleash that demon of addiction, which he'd managed to keep in check, and start to run riot. It took over with a vengeance; leaving a scene of despair, paranoia, open drawers, strewn clothes, ravaged bookshelves, and missing items.

Carl Manning had crossed that thin and delicate line that separates trust from betrayal. On this occasion, he wronged his good friend, who was now like a raging bull in a china shop.

A calming and somewhat soothing effect befell upon him the further he went inside the church. This was now between him and God. At least there was no need of lengthy explanations to his maker.

Inside the safety of the house of God, Manning started praying furiously. For the first time he felt his prayers had a special resonance – and that had nothing to do with the high ceilings of the church.

Pray the police find you before I do, Carl, because if I do, I will fucking kill you, you little piece of shit ... That last, chilling message he'd heard from Jack Parsons still resonated inside his head.

1998

Despite reaching this far, Kyra doubted she was a lucky girl. Two years of mental and emotional torture, besides the physical humiliation were taking their toll.

Although Kyra became used her current conditions, there was so much body and soul could endure without falling apart. She had already escaped one hell only to enter a new and more sinister one. Life was not meant to be this unfair.

Orphaned at a young age, she was thrown into state care at the lowest category because of her mixed background. The appointed officer's idea of state care was a young women's correctional institution near Chiang Mai, where he also happened to be the director.

She escaped the correctional institute in 1992 with a bittersweet outcome. Her cellmate and good friend, Priyanta, was not so lucky. Or probably she was – Priyanta was shot dead as they tried to escape to freedom. In hindsight, Kyra sometimes thought that Priyanta had earned her freedom through death.

Bangkok was a huge gamble for her. Parentless, without a Bhat to her name, and with a precarious identity, her options were quite limited. In fact, they were nil. Prostitution was an easy way out, especially with her exotic looks and at fifteen, she was probably in her prime.

After two years living on the streets, and despite all the precautions she had taken, Kyra succumbed to the dark side of the city and paid the price for her naivety. What seemed like the perfect choice of lifestyle turned out to be the worst possible nightmare.

She had reached the end of her endurance level. Kyra missed her mom and dad. The way things stood, death became her closest idea of paradise and peace.

Today, all that would change. Kyra had planned this moment for at least three weeks.

She had been awake since about three in the morning. It was almost five, and Claus would soon be home. Today, however, she would put an end to the abuse. Whatever the outcome, today was liberation day. Kyra only had this *one* opportunity.

She was convinced God would understand and have mercy on her. God was different to men like Claus. One or at most two matches would suffice.

With the right ingredients, fire usually travels fast.

COMING SOON
(STILL UNTITLED...)

i

Jake walked in front of his father, eager to catch a full glimpse of the Cutty Sark dressed up in full regalia. They were at the end of Greenwich Church street, merely yards away from The Gypsy Moth pub, the last obstacle to block the views of the former tea clipper.

National as well as maritime flags and banners hung from the masts in preparation for the celebrations, which were due to commence in the next 20 minutes.

'Hey sweetheart, not so fast!' Colin Barker yelled at Jake, his voice drowned by the music of a brass quintet performing just ten or twelve yards away from them. 'I told you to hold on to daddy, don't run.'

Jake slowed down as his eyes were glowing at the multi-colour display of flags, banners, the Cutty Sark, balloons, posters.

He turned round to his father: 'Daddy, buy me a balloon. A yellow one!'

Yellow is his favourite colour.

'But son, you're gonna loose it here with all these people.'

'Please ... I'll be your best friend.'

Colin had no heart to say no when Jake said that. He looked down at his six-year-old son. He couldn't believe how fast Jake was growing.

Jake had already shown from an early age a taste for everything maritime. The curtains in his room had anchors and knots patterns. Even his bed was shaped as a boat. In addition, he loved the beach.

'Can we can go on the ship daddy?'

'I'm not sure we can today darling, because of the celebrations, they might have it sealed off,' Colin explained as he kneeled down to tuck Jake's shirt back into his trousers. 'Anyway, we've already been inside twice; I'm sure there's nothing new today.'

'Aw, but it's so cool, daddy.'

Colin just nodded and grabbed his hand.

'Look, there's a man with lots of balloons,' Jake was not one to forget that easily when he wanted something.

Colin checked his wallet and grabbing Jake gently by the hand walked toward the balloon seller.

A healthy crowd had already gathered around the Cutty Sark. More people were sitting on the walls opposite the ship and near the entrance to the underground tunnel that crosses the river Thames. The brass band continued to play along. They were performing bluegrass versions of top chart hits from the likes of Adele, Rhianna, Robbie Williams, among others.

'How much for that yellow one you got up there,' Colin asked the balloon man, pointing at a *Spongebob Squarepants* yellow balloon that stood out from the rest.

'For young man her, two pound my friend,' replied balloon man with a thick Eastern European or Middle Eastern accent. The man was probably in his late thirties, clean-shaven, dead straight black hair that almost reached his shoulders.

Colin searched his right pocket for loose coins. When he finally felt he had two pounds he paid the man and grabbed the balloon for his son.

The excitement on Jake's face was priceless. His father finally handed him the balloon, while expertly tying the string around his left wrist to avoid it flying away.

Colin turned to thank the balloon man who gave a slight nod in gratitude.

Almost immediately, balloon man turned his head up to the sky. He then looked back down and checked his watch. After, he searched the left side of his shirt until he found what looked like a thin strap. He broadened his smile at Colin and Jake.

The smile turned into a sinister, teasing smirk as he violently pulled down the strap. Colin just about had enough time to grab hold of Jake and hug him.

'Yeah Geoff, can't believe I missed that gig yet again,' Captain Ronald McDowell retook the thread of the conversation once he had giving their position to the UK air traffic control after leaving Irish airspace. They were less than twenty-five minutes from London Gatwick now.

'A real shame Ron, it was actually quite good,' First Officer Geoffrey Tarrant was still checking one of the charts making sure the readings coincided with that displayed on the flight panel. 'Can't remember the name of the supporting band, they weren't too bad mind, but I won't be rushing to buy their CDs, let's put it that way.'

British Atlantic 422 please confirm position and switch to frequency 31.5,' squawked a male voice from Air Traffic Control.

Captain McDowell raised his brow at Geoff, shrugged his shoulders, and with a tired voice replied: 'British Atlantic 442, we are now 11,000 feet, turning right 5 degrees, heading over Chester, sir. Over.'

'Copy that, sir, thanks. Stay on course and maintain speed and altitude. Will update shortly. Over'

'Copy that. Thank you. Over.'

The flight had been mostly uneventful since leaving San Francisco just over nine and a half hours ago. A few bumpy moments while flying over the Canadian Rockies and the Labrador straits were as bad as it got. This was both McDowell's and Tarrant's tenth flight on the *Dreamliner*, although not necessarily together. They both had clocked up thousands of hours on the B777s and B767s, which were still British Atlantic's main fleet.

In a few moments, McDowell would be making the pre-landing announcement to the passengers and updating on their position as it was customary.

'I really do need to sort myself out on my days off. Missing Stereophonics live twice is unacceptable,' McDowell added, not too interested in knowing how much his First Officer had enjoyed the gig and he hadn't. For a second time.

'By the way, where you off to and what bird?' Tarrant asked, checking the speed and altitude readings.

'Seattle on Wednesday,' McDowell replied, fidgeting with his tie, 'on the old triple seven. This time I'm partnered with Tony Milligan.'

'Gosh! Haven't seen that miserable git in ages, how is he?'

'Usual, crazy as shit.'

'British Atlantic 422, please confirm position and start descent to 9.5. Over.'

'British Atlantic 422, we are northeast of Chester and will advise at 9.5. Starting descent now, over.'

'Copy that. Over.'

'And what about you Geoff?'

'Chicago on Thursday, and...' A hoarse-like roar ripped through the cabin.

'Oh fuck!' First Officer Tarrant felt the air being sucked out of his lungs as if a gigantic vacuum had been savagely plugged into his mouth. Hardly able to react, he barely managed to turn his head left, but all he saw was a huge gap where just seconds ago his captain used to sit. The deep dark blue sky looked vivid, crisp, and inviting.

UNDER CONSTRUCTION

ACKNOWLEDGMENTS

None of this would have been possible without a little help from my friends.

It is only fair I start by mentioning a few places in Lee that have served as impromptu and mobile offices. Luciano's Restaurant & Bar; The Kitchen, The Crown Pub, and last but by no means least, the Polish Tavern on Baring Road, where I officially launched my first book back in 2014.

Now for those made of flesh and soul. First, I must thank THE DAMNED, a dear and select group of conspirators, collaborators, and certified reprobates; Jessica Best, Paul Dibohu, and Alec Green. Thank you first for not sectioning me, and then agreeing to read my initial drafts, offering your thoughts, opinions and feedback on what and where to improve and still sparing me the embarrassment of what you had to read.

Niall Kervick, and Jesus Barrios for reviewing and offering sound feedback and suggestions on my final draft.

In addition to all this, a mega "thanks" to Jesus Barrios for designing the cover as well as detailing your vision for it. Lena Hedges, for your valuable editing, proofreading, synopsis and overall support. Łukasz Kamiński for your work on the back cover, sleeve and final touches before uploading. The difficult task of taking a decent picture of me to adorn said back cover goes to the lovely Aury Alonso.

The success of this collection will be all your fault!

The unsung heroes and villains, who have dashed in and out of my life and who some way or another, inspired me fully or partly on some of these stories, if you are reading this, you probably know who you are.

Now, a massive "thank-you" go to 48 fine people that believed and supported generously though the crowdfunding campaign to help get DAMNED IF I DON'T published. Without them, this would have almost been impossible or at the very least, a massive uphill task. A special mention however, goes to these fantastic people, who just went over and beyond: Gregorio Tomassi, Jason Marcellin, Judy Donovan, Mariela Mason, Xavier Fernandez, Betty Agostini, Fiona Clark, Nathaniel Nuby, Angela Peddar, Luc Agostini, Alec Green, Roberto Santana, Tania Mujica, Helen Plumb, Steve Agostini, Marshall Hughes, Sandy Clark, Jessica Best, Luis Fernandez, Erika Rath, A M Agostini-W, Neha Shah, Gloria Haynes, Debbie Foord, Simon Kraft, Lisa Mason, Will Hafod Dywyll, Niall Kervick.

Davıt Zmuda & Marek Dabrowski worked on the music, filming and direction of the promo clip of this book. You guys rock!

Indiegogo, for providing the crowdfunding platform to make it happen.

To CreateSpace, for offering the platform and the opportunity to terrorise the literary world with my book.

Finally, Marina and Alexander, because you are in my life.

ABOUT THE AUTHOR

Ant Richards was born at St. Mary Abbots Hospital in Kensington, London, but spent the formative part of his life in Caracas, Venezuela. For some reason unknown to the general public, the hospital no longer exists.

After finishing High School and clueless as to what he wanted to become professionally, Ant eventually heard the calling and trained as a recording engineer, working in leading dubbing and voiceover studios in his adopted hometown.

In the mid nineties, and looking to widen his horizons, Ant returned to his native London where he ended up working in the Travel Industry. Despite it no longer being the glamorous career it was portrayed to be, he was still able to indulge in his other passion; travelling.

Unable yet to become a millionaire and live the debonair lifestyle he craved, the dormant writing talent in him began to flourish. Or so he believed. At first, he thought it could be a rash.

For better or for worse, Ant Richards began his new career as an accomplished travel writer, reviewing destinations, accommodation, flights and other unrelated nonsense. However, despite his best efforts, he was still unable to enjoy the freebies and perks he rightfully thought he deserved after going through all the trouble.

It was only a matter of time before he seriously considered writing his first novel. After many failed attempts, years of solitary confinement (in pubs, cafes, airport lounges, hotel rooms... and more bars) IN YOUR DREAMS came to life, and terrorised the literary world, again with a varying degree of success - within his neighbourhood and local pub in Lee.

Ant Richards currently lives in South East London with his family. He supports Liverpool, therefore he is definitely a hopeless dreamer.

And if you haven't been deterred by this book or his bio, and still want to find out more about Ant Richards and his work, visit his website: www.antrichards.com

You can also follow him (at your own peril) on Facebook, twitter (@antrichards2014) & Instagram.

166

33859102R00099

Printed in Poland
by Amazon Fulfillment
Poland Sp. z o.o., Wrocław